Jason tried to explain about the girl, but Mom was in no mood to listen. "Oh, stop this nonsense, Jason," she snorted. "If you're going to invent excuses, at least make them vaguely believable! We were in the middle of the ocean. What would a girl be doing out there?"

"I don't know," he said defiantly. "But she was."

Mom was beginning to go red in the face. Winston walked over to Jason and muttered, "There is an old saying: When the tiger roars the wise rabbit flees."

Jason frowned. "And what does that mean?"

"It means get out while you still can," Winston said with a wink.

Jason took this advice and fled.

A little later he lay on his bunk, trying to figure it all out.

His thoughts were interrupted by Brett's teasing voice coming from the lower bunk. "There's one thing that explains it all, of course, Jace. You've finally gone totally crazy."

"I'm not crazy, you little nerd," Jason snarled through clenched teeth.

"That's what crazy people always say, though, isn't it?" Brett countered. He smirked to himself. It wasn't often he got the chance to stir Jason up this much.

For Ben, Kate, and Trish

First Hyperion Paperback edition 1995

Text © 1994 by Jonathan M. Shiff Productions Pty Ltd.
First published in 1994. Reprinted by permission of Mammoth Australia:
a part of Reed Books Australia.

Based on the television series of the same name
distributed by Beyond Distribution Party, Limited.

Printed in the United States of America.
1 3 5 7 9 10 8 6 4 2

Library of Congress Cataloging-in-Publication Data
Hepworth, Peter, date.
Ocean Girl / Peter Hepworth. – 1st Hyperion Paperback ed.
p.   cm.
Summary: Jason and Brett have their lives changed when they
discover a remote island paradise in the Great Barrier Reef, where
Ocean Girl swims with whales and understands what they say to her.
ISBN 0-7868-1070-X
1. Whales–Fiction. 2. Human-animal relationships–Fiction.
3. Great Barrier Reef (Qld.)–Fiction.] I. Title.
PZ7.H417Oc   1995
[Fic]–dc20   95-1189

The text for this book is set in 13-point Baskerville Book.

Designed by Lara S. Demberg.

OCEAN GIRL

PETER HEPWORTH

Hyperion Paperbacks for Children
New York

CONTENTS

ON THE DAY AFTER TOMORROW...

CHAPTER ONE
ORCA

The little island passing below them sat in the glittering sea of the Great Barrier Reef.

"Hey! Did the rest of you see that?"

Jason had to shout to be heard over the chattering of the helicopter's rotors above them. The pilot eased his headphones off one ear and glanced back over his shoulder.

"What, kid?"

"I thought I spotted something in a clearing back there. Like someone running across into the trees."

The pilot grinned in the way that adults do when they're about to treat you like an idiot. At fourteen, Jason had seen that look many times before.

"I think you need glasses, son. All these islands are uninhabited. Always have been. Way too far

1

from the mainland for anyone to want to live. You *ORCA* Institute people are going to be all on your own out here."

Jason pulled a face. "Oh, great," he groaned, and followed it up with a snorted, "Sheesh!"

Mom leaned over and gave him a cuff across the back of the head. She always said they were just playful, but sometimes they really hurt. They weren't so bad now that she no longer wore a wedding ring on that hand, though.

"Oh lighten up, Jason," she said. "Where's your sense of adventure?"

"Yeah. This is going to be cool!" Brett piped in. It was typical of his little brother. At ten years old, Brett still got excited no matter how dumb the place was that Mom was dragging them off to.

"Get real, will you?" Jason retorted, "Stuck in the middle of nowhere with a bunch of egghead scientists. You call that adventure?"

"Well, I really envy you boys," the pilot said. "To be actually living on the bottom of the sea! I'd give anything for a place on board *ORCA*."

"Well, you can have mine for nothing," Jason muttered, slumping back into his seat to stare gloomily out of the window. Ahead, the ocean stretched all around to the horizon, only broken here and there by tiny specks of land like the one they had just passed over. He glanced back at it as it quickly receded from view. Funny. For a moment there, he really thought he had seen someone. Just a glimpse of a little figure that paused, stared up at them, and then disappeared quickly beneath the thick foliage.

No, he decided. It couldn't have been. And he pushed the thought from his mind.

✳   ✳

Neri stepped from the cover of the rainforest canopy back into the clearing. She watched the flying machine go with both fear and fascination. Its roar faded as it dwindled to a dot and disappeared from view. That had been too close. Though she had seen them in the sky nearly every day since the Outsiders started building the strange thing in the sea, they rarely flew directly over the island. So this one had caught her by surprise. She must never make that mistake again.

From the day she was left alone, she decided the Outsiders must not know about her.

Or about the giant in the ocean. Jali. Her friend.

✳   ✳

"Jeez, she's really done it this time," Jason hissed out of the corner of his mouth. "What is this dump, Devil's Island?"

The helicopter had lifted above their heads and was already swinging away back in the direction of the mainland. They stood with a jumble of bags and suitcases in piles around their feet, still clutching their caps against the buffeting of the downdraft.

Jason surveyed the scene with dismay. It was even worse than he had anticipated. Back on shore, Mom had tried to make it sound as if *ORCA* was the next best thing to Disneyland. What confronted them now was a vast, ugly, gray metal platform sitting alone in endless ocean. Boats of varying sizes bobbed at moorings alongside. The only thing that broke the dreary flatness of the platform itself was a large cylindrical structure in the middle. On its front was a symbol and the words OCEANIC RESEARCH CENTER (AUSTRALIA).

Mom walked toward it, looking rapt.

"I'm working out some way to get us off here fast!" Jason hissed to Brett.

"I heard that, Jason," Mom said without turning. Her voice was calm but there was a note of warning in it.

They were interrupted by a soft whooshing sound. A door was sliding open in the side of the large central cylinder. A figure emerged, a small, sprightly man whose huge grin split dark Indian features. He was dressed in a blue uniform with the *ORCA* crest emblazoned on a top pocket.

"Hello, Dr. Bates," he hailed Mom. "How was the flight?"

"Fine, thanks, Winston." She motioned the boys forward. "Boys, my research assistant, Dr. Seth. This is . ."

"Jason? And this one, Brett, right?" he guessed correctly. "Welcome to *ORCA*!"

"Yeah," Jason replied flatly, "you're welcome to it, too."

Winston shot a look at Jason, one eyebrow cocked, before he plunged into the pile of luggage and began loading himself up with bags. Brett hurried to help him. They began to carry them toward the open door in the cylinder.

As they did, Winston fell in step beside Jason. "You know, Jason," he said quietly, "there is a very wise old Japanese saying: The carp smiles on the surface, for he has seen the wonders below." And he gestured downward under their feet.

"What's that supposed to mean?" Jason challenged.

"How should I know? I'm Indian," Winston said with a high-pitched giggle that continued as he led them through the doorway.

They found themselves in a circular elevator with one large seat running most of the way around it. Winston dropped the bags he was carrying and fished a handful of plastic cards from his pocket. He passed these in turn across a sensor plate on a panel by the door. After each there was a beep and then the words SECURITY CLEARANCE flashed across a screen above.

"Your identity cards," Winston explained, handing them out. "You must wear them at all times. You cannot get in or out without them."

Brett's eyes were shining with excitement as he pinned the card to his shirt. "Dr. Seth," he asked, "is it true there's like a whole city down there?"

"Well, more a large town, I'd say, Brett. But

you'll find it has everything we need." He took a seat as the door began to slide shut.

"Has it got a McDonald's?" Jason asked.

Winston blinked in surprise. "No," he confessed.

Jason nudged Brett. "I told you," he grunted. "We might as well be going back to the Stone Age."

With a gentle hum, they began to descend.

✳   ✳

Neri knelt in the heart of the rainforest, clawing sweet young yams from the ground and eating them on the spot.

Then suddenly, she heard the call. Faint, from way out to sea. Her friend was coming. She stood and, still chewing, began to head toward the beach.

✳   ✳

The elevator doors opened.

"Welcome to the *ORCA* Maritime Research Station," cooed a female robot voice issuing from speakers overhead. "Would all new arrivals please report to the Berth Allocation Terminal located directly to your left."

"That's HELEN, our central computer," Winston explained as they began to shuffle out with their bags. "Short for Hydro Electronic Liaison Entity Number 3000. She really runs this place. But don't ever tell the commander I said that," he added with a nervous giggle.

Nearby was a model of the *ORCA* complex in a glass case, its cluster of modules with connecting

6

tubes looking like some nest of strange, gigantic shellfish linking arms on the bottom of the sea. Winston led them past it to where another sensor plate jutted from the wall and told them to lay their ID cards on it.

"Please wait while your cabin details are confirmed." It was the same mechanical woman's voice, but this time coming from a speaker on the wall.

Jason and Brett took in the scene around them as they waited. They were in a large-domed reception area from which tunnel-like corridors seemed to run off in every direction. It was clearly some kind of central hub, judging by the number of people constantly passing through. A lot were adults, but there seemed to be a good many kids of various ages, too. All wore uniforms with the *ORCA* symbol prominently displayed.

"Bates . . . Dr. Dianne Elizabeth . . . Jason David . . . Brett Michael," the voice broke in again. "Residency clearance. Your berth allocation is Gamma module, level three, cabin fourteen. Have a nice day."

Winston began to lead them toward one of the tunnels, but paused to speak to a tall, hawk-faced man with gold braid on his uniform.

"Ah, Commander Lucas, may I introduce Dianne Bates. Dr. Bates is one of our leading marine biologists. She's here to study the songs of humpback whales."

"Dr. Bates," the man said, nodding to Mom. But his eyes were firmly fixed on Jason and Brett. "Are these two yours?"

"Yes."

He glared at them. "Well, just remember this is a vessel at sea as far as I'm concerned, not a kindergarten or a playground. Obey orders, don't mess about, and you'll have no trouble, Doctor." He nodded curtly again in Mom's direction before turning on his heel and walking off.

"Oh, this is just great!" Jason moaned as they continued on their way. "We've signed on with Captain Bligh."

They followed through a series of gently winding narrow corridors and voice-operated elevators. At one point, the gray metal walls gave way to thick pressure-proof glass and they found themselves standing in a viewing tunnel, from which they could look out at the seabed spread before them. Permanently lit by great banks of lights, the *ORCA* structure stood perched on the edge of the continental shelf, beyond which everything disappeared into permanent darkness.

The cabin was small, awfully small. Hardly the size of the little study Dad had back home when they'd all lived together. Against one wall was a cubicle the size of a telephone booth which appeared to be a toilet until Jason tried to find the flush button on the control panel. He emerged, wet and spluttering, to announce that it was also the shower, obviously designed by an idiot.

Against another wall stood a giant screen, which Winston explained was the internal communications system. "If you wish to talk to your mother up in our laboratory—or if she wishes to contact you—all you need do is punch in the number and you can talk to her face-to-face," he said enthusiastically. "Although, of course, you can push the nonvision button so she can't see what mischief you're really up to."

He was about to demonstrate, but the boys were already examining the sleeping berths. One led off to either side. They were identical. A double bunk and no room for much else. Since one had to be Mom's, obviously that meant they were to share. Two *ORCA* outfits lying side by side, still wrapped in plastic, confirmed it.

Mom followed them to the doorway.

"Well, time to get out of those street clothes and into uniform," she said cheerfully.

Brett already had the wrapping off his, but Jason turned defiantly. "No way, Mom, I'm not walking around looking like some geek space cadet. No way, no how."

"Orders, Jason," she said with that look in her eye that meant she was serious. "And then, we can all go up together while Winston shows me our new lab."

Brett was actually parading around, showing off his outfit to Mom, when Jason finally emerged, reluctantly wearing the cotton trousers and T-shirt with the *ORCA* symbol.

Winston had news for Dianne as they headed out the door. "I think I've already picked out our specimen. A big humpback who's been hanging around the area since I arrived to set our equipment up."

Jason could see the flash of excitement in Mom's eyes. Funny. She often got like that about work, but hardly ever about anything that happened at home. Perhaps that's why Dad . . .

"Don't worry. It always takes newcomers a few days to settle in here, but you'll get used to it." He realized Winston had dropped back and was walking beside him.

"I don't want to stay long enough to get used to it," Jason replied, looking straight ahead, "and I sure didn't ask to come. I just got dragged along to bag you guys a whale."

✳   ✳

Neri stood on the beach, staring out to sea.

Suddenly, the water at the mouth of the cove in front of her shimmered and then erupted as Jali's great body broke the surface, and a plume of spray jetted into air. She heard his voice, singing in her head.

I have returned, Neri.

She ran into the sea and plunged beneath the waves. One, two, three powerful kicks and she was zooming through the coral groves at high speed. Shoals of rainbow-colored fish darted des-

10

perately out of her way as she plowed through them. She surfaced beside the huge head and ran a hand under his eye, stroking him in welcome.

Come. Time to play, he sang, and he started to dive. Neri waited until he was nearly submerged. Only his tail remained out of the water, towering above her head. Then she, too, dived.

His giant flukes dwarfed her little feet as both slid under the surface. Then, together, they turned back out toward the open sea.

❉   ❉

Jason lay in bed that night listening to Brett's regular breathing from the bunk below. Sometimes he wondered if Mom didn't have a bit of a screw loose. He knew it was true humpback whales sang to each other underwater. Everyone knew that. But she had this idea that if you recorded the song and the whale's brain waves at the same time, you could eventually work out why the whale made certain sounds. Sooner or later, you'd be able to understand their language.

"You never know, Jason," she said once. "Some day we might actually be able to talk to them."

That was the crazy idea which had led to them being stuck in this hole for the next six months.

Jason snorted and rolled over to go to sleep. People talking to whales, he thought drowsily. Yeah, sure, Mom. In your dreams.

In your dreams.

CHAPTER TWO
THE HUNT

Jason nursed the crossbow in the crook of his arm as he double-checked the safety harness that secured him to the prow of the boat. He had reason to be cautious. Though the powerful craft was just cruising through the water now, he knew things would be different when the chase began. He could easily slip overboard if not firmly anchored to the deck.

He adjusted the bow's sights. Despite himself, he was beginning to feel a rush of excitement. They had waited nearly a week before the target whale had been spotted again. Now at last he was about to put all the months of boring practice to the test.

The commander had nearly ruined everything. He'd really made a scene about Jason being only fourteen and the bow being a lethal weapon. Mom had shown him the certificate proving that Jason had finished the safety course in proper handling.

"His instructor rated Jason as the best young marksman he'd ever trained," she'd pointed out, offering to match him against anyone else on *ORCA*.

It was only after a lot of argument that the commander had finally given in. And even then he'd insisted that no one else was to be near Jason while he had the bow in his hands.

Back in the wheelhouse, Brett watched as Mom and Winston hovered over a screen.

"This won't actually hurt the whale, will it?" he asked.

"Of course not, Brett," Mom said, a bit annoyed. "It's just like a little dart. He won't feel more than a pin prick, I promise."

"Well, we'll feel a darned sight more than a pin prick if we run into anything out here!" the boat's skipper snorted. He had been grumbling since they left *ORCA*. Mom and Winston had packed so much equipment into the wheelhouse, he complained, that he could scarcely see forward at all.

Mom calmly reminded him that a collision was not very likely in midocean. Besides, their advanced Lanar tracking system would give ample warning of anything ahead, above, or below the water. They were interrupted by Winston's shout.

"I've picked him up!"

Brett hurried over. Winston's finger was pointing to a fuzzy shape on the screen. "Due east. Right where the spotter planes said."

Mom reached for a headset. "Jason?"

Her voice squawked through the earphones of the matching headset Jason wore. He pulled the mouthpiece up into position. "Yeah?"

"We're on his track. Better load up."

Jason picked up the dart. It was not much larger than his hand, the barbed head studded with tiny transmitters and sensors. He clicked it into place in the bow.

Twenty minutes later, they found the whale, lolling on the surface of the water. Cutting back the engines, they edged slowly and steadily toward him. Jason half lifted the bow. This is going to be too easy, he thought.

Suddenly the whale arched and, in one rolling action, began to move away, picking up speed.

Mom's voice crackled through the earphones. "He's seen us. He's making a run for it. Hang on, Jason!"

With a powerful roar, the boat shot forward.

Jason was thrown around in the harness as the boat buffeted through the water, giving chase. Spray flew over the prow, blinding him. The animal desperately tried to change course, but it was no match for the throbbing engines and before long they were on his tail and closing.

The call burst into Neri's brain like a flash of lighting. *Danger. There is danger.*

A moment later, she saw the vision. The churned-up ocean. The vessel bearing relentlessly down. The Outsider on the front of it with the weapon in his hands.

She raced into the water and streaked out toward the open sea.

I am coming, my friend. I am coming.

✳ ✳

The boat sat nearly motionless in the water. The whale had dived, but Jason knew they would be monitoring his movements underwater back in the wheelhouse. Now it was just a matter of being in the right place when he surfaced.

"Aww, Mom, can't I go out and watch?" Brett begged.

She glanced up from the screen which she and Winston were craning over. "No. You heard what the commander said, Brett. You stay here."

Brett pulled face. Why did parents always want to stop kids from having a good time?

"He's coming up!" Winston cried. "Almost dead ahead, just to the left."

"Port," the skipper corrected as he swung the wheel, his eyes glued to the screen. The engines churned.

"Here he comes, Jason," Mom said into the mouthpiece of her headset, "right in front of you."

15

"Yeah, I've got him." On the prow, Jason could see the huge dark shape rising to the surface.

He cocked the bow and lifted it as the creature's bulk began to break the waterline.

"Stand by to fire and confirm."

"Right."

He hefted the bow to his shoulder, running through the instructions one last time. Near the blowhole. Behind that part of the head where the brain was located. As the creature seemed to pause for a moment, he lined up the spot in his sights, slipped the safety catch with his thumb and held his breath.

The whale was almost stationary. At this range, he couldn't miss. His finger tightened on the trigger.

And then a girl appeared, out of nowhere, thrusting up from the depths at incredible speed. She burst to the surface right in his line of fire. Between him and the whale. Her arms splayed out defensively as she screamed against the noise of the motors: "NO!"

Jason froze, his jaw dropping.

"Now, Jason! Fire and confirm." There was a rising urgency in Mom's voice through the earphones, but Jason could neither speak nor move. He just stood there, gaping at the girl. There was no land in sight. No other boat to be seen. Where had she come from? How did she get there?

The girl met his gaze steadily. There was a pleading in her sea green eyes, but also anger. The force

16

of that look was such that Jason did not feel capable of tearing his own eyes away. Beyond her, he was vaguely aware of ripples starting to spread.

"For heaven's sake, he's starting to move again! Fire, Jason, fire!"

But Jason was transfixed.

The girl seemed to hear the running footsteps before he did. Her eyes flicked toward the stern of the boat, then, in a flash, she flipped and dived, slipping out of sight at the same speed she had arrived.

The next thing Jason was aware of, Mom was at his side, ripping the crossbow from his hands. "Give me that." Her voice was shaking with fury.

She spun around, steadied herself, aimed and fired.

The whale was preparing to submerge again. Normally, Mom couldn't hit the side of a barn but, by some miracle, the dart flew straight and true. It struck just in front of the blowhole a moment before it disappeared under the water.

"Oh, my—I hit it." For a moment, her voice was a hushed whisper, but not for long. She rounded on Jason, eyes blazing. "All right, what happened? Why didn't you fire?"

"There was a girl." Even as he said it, Jason was aware of how pathetic it sounded.

"There . . . was . . . what?"

"A girl. In the ocean. She . . . she just appeared. And she was in the way."

17

With dangerous calm, Mom indicated the unbroken waterline to the horizon. "Well where is she now, then, Jason?"

Jason shrugged helplessly. "I don't know."

Winston had come up to join them, with Brett trailing on his heels. Jason appealed to them. "Didn't anyone else see that girl that was in the water?"

They stared at him blankly.

Mom ignored him. She turned to Winston, businesslike. "I think I might have lucked out, Winston. But we'll have to get back to the lab to be sure. Ask him to head for *ORCA* straightaway, will you?"

Winston gave Jason a strange look before heading back toward the wheelhouse.

"As for you, young man," Mom added to Jason, "we're going to be having a very long talk, believe me." She followed Winston.

"But, Mom," Jason called after her, "there was a girl. She was there."

Mom just kept walking. Brett stood, grinning at his older brother, twirling one finger around his ear. "Sure she was. And so were the Easter Bunny and the Tooth Fairy, right?"

Jason looked out at the empty sea, bewildered. "I saw her," he said to himself.

"Jace," Brett's voice came from behind him, "this time you're really up the creek."

The engines fired up as the boat began to come around to head for home.

18

Neri's head came up out of the water. The boat was in the distance now, heading away at speed. She watched it go, troubled.

Back in the laboratory the equipment on the tag all seemed to be working perfectly, to Jason's relief. On one screen, a glowing blip registered the location of the whale at that moment. At the same time, another monitor showed the repeating patterns of his brain waves. Winston calculated that both could be picked up within a range of twelve miles. And all the time, the sound of whale songs issued from two speakers. The whole room rang with strange whistles, moans, and squeals, relayed by the powerful transmitters.

"Listen to that, Winston," Mom cried jubilantly, "I've never heard any others so clearly. Quick, let's start recording straightaway!"

Brett hurried to help set up the recorder. Only Jason stood aside from the excitement, knowing his mother would turn her attention back to him sooner or later. He didn't have long to wait.

"You realize this is no thanks to you, Jason," she said sharply. "That little stunt of yours could have set our work back by weeks."

Jason tried to protest, but she overrode him.

"Ever since I accepted this position, you've been sulking. I've put up with it because you were having to give up a lot of things back onshore—

including the occasional weekend you got to spend with your father. . . ."

For a moment, her voice softened at the mention of Dad. Then it quickly hardened again. " . . . But to deliberately try to ruin this project just because you don't like being here is unforgivable!"

"I didn't . . ."

"Don't you think I know what was going on in your mind? Mess up the tagging and maybe we'd all get sent home, right?"

"No!"

"Then why didn't you fire when you were told?"

Again Jason tried to explain about the girl, but Mom was in no mood to listen. "Oh, stop this nonsense, Jason," she snorted. "If you're going to invent excuses, at least make them vaguely believable! We were in the middle of the ocean. What would a girl be doing out there?"

"I don't know," he said defiantly. "But she was."

Mom was beginning to go red in the face. Winston walked over to Jason and muttered, "There is an old saying: When the tiger roars, the wise rabbit flees."

Jason frowned. "And what does that mean?"

"It means get out while you still can," Winston said with a wink.

Jason took this advice and fled.

A little later he lay on his bunk, trying to figure it all out. Clearly, no one else had seen the girl, but that was not surprising when he thought about it.

They would all have been watching either their equipment or the whale. And even if they had looked, he was on the bow, blocking their view. So they only had his word. And none of them believed it.

His thoughts were interrupted by Brett's teasing voice coming from the lower bunk. "There's one thing that explains it all, of course, Jace. You've finally gone totally crazy."

"I'm not crazy, you little nerd," Jason snarled through clenched teeth.

"That's what crazy people always say, though, isn't it?" Brett countered. He smirked to himself. It wasn't often he got the chance to stir Jason up this much.

Jason swung down from the bunk and faced his little brother angrily. "Listen, I did see a girl, bozo. I don't know how and I don't know why—but she has to be out there somewhere, and I'm going to prove it."

Jason's face was stony. Even Brett was aware of a strange determination in his voice. "I'll show you all," he said quietly, "if I have to stay here for the rest of my life. I'm not leaving now until I find her."

CHAPTER THREE
THE STORM

H ey, you didn't say anything to anybody?" Jason grabbed Brett's arm as they were about to enter the Lyceum, a large cabin full of computer screens that served as their classroom.

"Huh?"

Jason dropped his voice to a whisper. "About what I saw, you know. I don't want the whole world thinking I'm loony. You didn't tell any of those little dorky friends of yours, did you?"

Brett's eyes opened in a look of pained innocence. "Hey, I'm your brother, Jace. Would I do something like that?"

The minute they stepped through the door there was an eruption of laughter and missiles. Balls of wadded-up computer paper rained down on Jason to a chorus of catcalls from the entire class.

"Hey, Bates, seen any more mermaids today?"

"Why didn't you bring her sister back for me?"

"I'll have one in batter—with a dollar's worth of chips!"

Jason glared at Brett. "I'll get even with you for this," he said, grimly.

✳   ✳

As it turned out he never did get even with Brett. It was Vanessa Lane who did and for an entirely different reason.

Vanessa was one of those freckled, carroty-haired girls who acted as if she was doing you a favor by letting you breathe the same air she did. She'd only been on board *ORCA* three days, but that was long enough to get on just about everybody's nerves. So it wasn't really surprising that Brett decided she deserved the old initiation trick.

It was pretty simple to play. Most new people on board forgot you had to turn off the vision on the communications screen if you wanted privacy. Otherwise callers could see straight into your cabin. So, all you had to do was wait until they were in a really embarrassing situation and then dial up their number.

They got Vanessa when she was in the shower cubicle. Brett had two accomplices, kids he'd got friendly with. One was Froggy, a little guy who was supposed to be a real whiz with computers. The other was a girl called Zoe, a tomboy with a

23

permanent scowl. It was Zoe who actually rang the bell before bolting away down the corridor to join the others.

By the time Vanessa answered the door, dripping wet and with a towel clutched in front of her, there was no one in sight. She was actually leaning out the door, peering down the corridor, when she became aware of the watching figures on the screen behind her, applauding the unprotected view from behind.

"Looking good, Vanessa," Brett observed.

She mightn't have taken it so hard if Froggy hadn't patched it into the public viewing areas. For a few glorious moments, all the kids in the galley and recreation rooms were treated to the sight of Vanessa's frantic efforts to cover her freckled backside.

From her point of view, of course, all she could see were the three faces on the screen.

"Welcome to *ORCA*, sucker!"

The three of them said it in unison, but it was Brett's face Vanessa had seen most clearly. Even before the screen went to black a moment later, she had sworn she would pay him back, and it wasn't long before she got her chance.

A few days later Brett was alone up on the platform topside. One of the new ANT (Automatic Navigation Transport) boats was being dismantled for servicing, and he had taken advantage of the mechanic's absence to poke around inside the little

24

craft. Vanessa crept up behind him, slipped the mooring rope and, with a mighty shove, pushed it clear of the platform. By the time Brett realized what had happened, he was sixteen feet away and drifting further out to sea.

"What do you think you are doing? How am I supposed to get back?" Brett yelled.

"Looks like you're going to have to swim, doesn't it?" Vanessa called. Then with a final "So, welcome to *ORCA*, sucker!" she hurried back to the elevator and disappeared below.

Brett considered the possibilities. He certainly wasn't going to give Vanessa the satisfaction of seeing him walk back inside dripping wet. No, he decided, he would work out how to start the unfamiliar craft and then steer it back to its moorings. He started to push controls at random, which was a mistake.

With a sudden roar, the engines burst into life. The boat took off with a surge of power that knocked Brett off his feet and sent him tumbling. He lay in the bottom of the boat, stunned.

By the time he recovered and looked back over the stern, the *ORCA* platform was more than six hundred feet away and disappearing rapidly, and he was rocketing, out of control, toward the open sea.

✳   ✳

On her island, Neri heard the warning call from out to sea and looked up. One glance at the gath-

25

ering clouds and strange light in the sky told her that her friend was right. There was a big wind coming.

She moved through the forest, picking handfuls of berries of different colors, but avoiding the bright yellow ones that grew on the banks of the stream.

"Badberries," she muttered to herself and moved on.

When she had collected what she needed, she climbed hand over hand up the tree that held her sleeping nest at the top. She settled down, put the berries where she could easily reach them, and began to lash herself to the trunk with vines.

Then she settled down to wait out the big wind.

✳   ✳

The waves around *ORCA* were already starting to wash over the platform when Jason realized something was wrong.

He was sitting in the galley with a group of kids he'd started to hang around with. There was goofy-looking Damien Arthur Geoffries, who, because of his personality as much as his unfortunate initials, was known to everyone as "Daggy." Beside him sat Jodie, her face dotted with antipimple cream under teased blond hair, her nose stuck in a copy of *Seventeen* magazine. And there was also a quiet but pretty girl named Lee. Jason had liked Lee from the first moment he met her. It had come as a bad shock when Daggy told him Lee was

Commander Lucas's daughter.

"If he ever thought you were giving her the eye, you'd be a dead duck," Daggy warned, drawing a finger across his throat.

Jason was surprised to see his mother approaching. Normally, the kids had the galley to themselves until adults started to drift in for their evening meal.

"Jason, have you or any of your friends seen Brett around? I can't find him anywhere," Mom looked worried.

Vanessa chimed in from another table, "I think I saw him up top fooling around in one of the boats," she said innocently. "But that was ages ago."

That's when they found out that one of the automatic navigation boats was missing.

Half an hour later, Commander Lucas was raging around the control bridge. "For heaven's sake, woman, can't you people even keep track of your own children!" he thundered, as he issued orders for search boats to be sent out.

"Don't worry, Mom, they'll find him." Jason tried to sound reassuring, but Lucas scowled at him.

"I think you'll have to face a few hard facts," he said flatly. "First, we don't have any idea how far he may have gone or in which direction. Second, we have a tropical cyclone about to hit this area like an express train in half an hour. When that happens, I'll have to call the searchers in. I can't risk their lives."

"Then I'll take a boat and go and look for him myself," Mom replied.

"Try that and I'll have you locked in the brig for your own safety," Lucas barked. Then he added, more quietly, "Look, it's a very seaworthy little vessel and, for all we know, he may have reached the safety of land already. But if we don't find him, I give you my word I'll have a full-scale operation ready to go at first light."

Exactly forty-five minutes later, with the light fading, the search was called off.

✳   ✳

Brett clung to the gunwales of the tiny craft as it was flung about in the mountainous seas. The boat had kept going until it ran out of fuel and now Brett didn't have the slightest idea where he was. All he knew was that he was in bad trouble.

"Mom! Mom!" he yelled desperately, but the howling winds simply snatched his words and hurled them back in his face.

BRETT AND BADBERRIES

B y next morning the cyclone had passed and the
search was resumed. When Jason looked at the
size of the search area, the endless miles of sea
around them, he felt his heart start to sink.

"If only the communication system hadn't been
dismantled for servicing, we could have got a fix
on him," Lucas muttered as he studied his chart.
He glanced across to Jason. "Do you know if he
had any water with him?"

"No—at least I don't think so," Jason muttered,
unhappily.

"Pity. It's shaping to be a hot day," Lucas
returned to his chart. "Anything out there in an
open boat's going to start cooking."

The sun was high and blazing in the sky. It was nearing midafternoon, though Brett lost all sense of time. His head was spinning, his mouth was parched, and he would have given even the treasured laser-blades he'd had to leave back onshore for just one glass of water.

The boat had been drifting aimlessly with the currents since he woke that morning. At first, he was grateful to have survived, but as the day drew on and the sun grew hotter, he began to wonder if what he faced wasn't even more horrible than drowning. In the end, he simply curled up in the stern of the boat and went to sleep.

He was awakened only when the boat shuddered as the prow struck sand and ground to a halt. Brett sat up and stared around him.

He had run aground on a beautiful white beach that seemed to stretch as far as his bleary eyes could see. He hoped that it might be the mainland, gut there were no signs of houses or any other buildings anywhere around.

He slipped over the side, fell into the water, and waded unsteadily ashore. "Hello! Is there anybody here?" He yelled as hard as his aching throat would allow.

There was no reply.

"Please help me! I need water!"

Again there was no answer, just the screeching of birds in the forest that bordered the beach. Not knowing what else to do, Brett staggered toward the trees.

He was near collapse when he came upon a stream running through the forest. He didn't even notice the small ring of stones, burnt black from many cooking fires, that stood nearby. He simply rushed past it and threw himself face first into the water, gulping it down. It was sweet and cool and he drank deeply.

His thirst finally slaked, Brett suddenly realized he was hungry, too. Maddeningly hungry. He peered hopefully around for something to eat and he saw some yellow berries on the bank.

They were plump and inviting, and when he bit unsurely into the first one, his mouth was filled with a taste like Christmas pudding. A little moldy, perhaps, but Christmas pudding, nevertheless. He started to grab them by the handful, stuffing them into his mouth, not minding the yellow juice that stained his lips, trickled down his chin, and dripped onto the ground below.

He was still collecting them when a strange feeling started to come over him. Everything began to blur then the forest around him seemed to start to move in a circle, slowly at first, then faster and faster. At the same time, his whole body went numb.

Brett fell headlong and the world went black.

✳   ✳

The moment she surfaced in the cove, Neri saw

the boat on the beach. For a moment she froze, her fingers tightening on the fishing spear she carried. A small grouper was transfixed on the barbed point, still trembling. Then she began to wade ashore, moving warily toward the strange vessel.

She circled it slowly, and found a line of footprints leading away toward the forest.

An Outsider. There was an Outsider on her island!

Neri moved like a shadow through the undergrowth, slipping from the shelter of one tree to another, following the tracks. She had nearly reached the place she called home when she came upon a figure sprawled on the bank of the stream.

She leaned over the unmoving form, frowning at the strange clothes and the ugly black things tied onto his feet. Shoes, she remembered, that's what her father had said they were called.

She peered closer to see the creature's face and spotted the yellow stains on his lips. She knew instantly that he had eaten badberries.

She paused for only a second then dashed into the surrounding forest, where she began to gather the plants she needed.

❋   ❋

Brett woke to feel something being pressed against his lips. It was a cup made from half a coconut shell, filled with some evil-smelling brew. He tried to push it away.

"Drink."

Brett opened his eyes and started. The face he looked into was that of a girl a little older than himself. A matted mane of sun-bleached hair framed a broad forehead, straight nose, and full mouth. But it was her eyes that commanded attention; they were like the ocean, sea green and wild. Even in the semidarkness, they seemed to glitter in their sockets.

The girl was tall and slender but there was a sense of hidden strength in her lithe, bronzed limbs. She wore a simple dress made of some strange, rough fabric the like of which Brett had never seen. The hem had rotted away in places leaving a tangle of threads halfway up her thigh.

She pushed the cup to his mouth again.

As she lifted his head, Brett became aware of a large seashell full of liquid bubbling away over a nearby fire.

"You eat badberries," she said. "Drink. Or you go away forever."

The urgent look on her face suddenly made Brett's blood cold. "You don't mean . . . die?"

She seemed to consider this for a moment, then shrugged and nodded.

The liquid had a strange salty taste to it. Before he had even finished the cup, Brett felt a soothing warmth begin to travel through his entire body. His eyelids started to droop.

"You sleep now," the girl said. "Be better soon."

She laid his head back down, but remained

crouched over him. Brett heard his own voice as though coming from somewhere far away. "Who are you? What's your name?"

One corner of her mouth tilted in the slightest flicker of a smile. "Neri," she said.

✳ ✳

Brett woke from a fitful sleep several times during the night, but she was always there. Mostly she just squatted silently nearby, staring at him with a puzzled look on her face. Once he caught her holding her hand against his, as though comparing the two. In the darkest hours, he was dimly aware of her soothing his brow with water while she crooned a strange little tune of squeaks and chirping sounds under her breath. It sounded oddly familiar to Brett, but he was already slipping back into sleep when it occurred to him where he had heard something like it before.

In his mother's lab.

It was the sound of whales singing.

✳ ✳

It was shortly after sunup next morning when Winston, on one of the search boats, reported spotting something in the sea at a distance.

On *ORCA*, Mom clutched Jason's hand tightly.

A minute or two later Winston came back on screen to correct himself. On drawing closer, they had realized the object was a whale, basking in the water.

"From the fluke marks, it looks like it might

34

even be our chap," he added distractedly.

Lucas broke in, telling them to move on to the next search area.

As the boat altered course, the whale watched them go. Then it began to sing.

✳   ✳

"Boy! Boy!"

Brett awoke to find Neri shaking him. He still felt weak and awfully tired, and he tried to roll back over to sleep, but she persisted. "Boy! Your name?"

"Brett," he mumbled.

"Bre-ett." She tried it out to herself experimentally before beginning to shake him again. "Brett, your people look for you. Don't want coming here to my island. Take you to where they find. Now."

But Brett just lay there. He simply didn't feel strong enough to move. So Neri bent over him. With one hoist, she lifted him bodily off the ground as if he were a rag doll. Then, holding him in her arms, she headed for the beach.

She placed him in the boat, then paused. Brett was aware of her eyes boring into him. "Brett, I must have promise. Tell none about me. You swear."

"I swear."

She nodded, stepped to the front of the boat and seized the mooring rope. Brett gasped as he felt the craft move. The girl was single-handedly pulling the boat back into the water!

Then, when it was floating free, she slid under the surface of the sea. The rope tightened again and the boat began to move forward. Slowly at first, then gathering speed, as she towed it away from the island and out toward the open ocean.

*   *

Winston's excited face flashed onto the communicator screen. "We've found him! He's a little the worse for wear, but they say he'll be fine."

Mom hugged Jason. He could see she was blinking back tears and he felt a lump forming in his own throat. He'd never admit it to Brett—he didn't let on about his feelings to anyone these days—but he couldn't imagine life without the little dork.

"It's very strange," Winston went on, scratching his head. "We searched through here an hour ago and there was no sign of him. Suddenly, there he is, just floating right in front of us. We don't know where he came from."

In the background Brett was being lifted aboard the search ship on a stretcher. Winston stepped over to him. "How are you feeling, my boy?" he asked kindly.

Brett looked up, fuzzily. "Where's Neri?"

Winston's brow wrinkled. "Neri? What is Neri?"

Then Brett remembered his promise. "Nothing," he replied. "Just a dream."

*   *

That evening, back in his own bunk, Brett lay

silently thoughtful for a long time before he finally spoke. "Jace, I met her."

"Met who?" Jason asked without interest.

"The girl in the sea. The one you saw. In fact, I think she saved my life."

Jason swung down from the top bunk, his eyes wide with excitement. "You're kidding!"

"Uh-huh," Brett said, and told him the whole story. Jason listened, hanging on every word.

"Do you think you could find the island again?" he asked when Brett had finished.

Brett shook his head. "I don't have the faintest idea where I was. And listen, Jace, you've got to keep all this to yourself. I gave my word. I'm only telling you because, well, you kinda knew about her already."

"Hey, after the scolding I got last time, I'm not saying anything," Jason pointed out. "Not until we can actually show 'em this Neri in the flesh. And that day's going to be worth waiting for."

FACE-TO-FACE

They were out in midocean when they finally met Neri face-to-face again. Jason had just gained his boat license and, as part of his probation, had been sent to mark an illegal drift net for destruction. These nets swept the seas with their mesh, trapping not only fish but all other marine life as they went.

They had already freed two turtles and a young dolphin when Brett noticed the bubbles further along the line, bubbles that meant something else was caught in the cruel web below. Jason slipped on a mask and snorkel and went down for a look, and there she was.

She had been trying to free an old lady turtle and in doing so got her own legs entangled in the drifting tendrils. The more she tried to kick herself free, the more they wrapped around her.

Jason drew the knife that was strapped to his ankle, sucked in a lungful of air and kicked down toward her. He came up behind the girl and began to slash at the net, cutting both her and the turtle free.

She spun around in surprise. Then she saw the knife. Before Jason could react, she was gone. With one kick of her legs, she shot away at an incredible speed into the depths. Jason could only gape.

"She was down there!" he gasped breathlessly as he hauled himself back on to the deck.

"I know," Brett said with maddening calmness. He pointed. Neri had returned. Her head and shoulders bobbed in the water a little way off.

"Hey, Neri!" Brett yelled, waving. "Remember me?"

"Bre-ett," Neri answered. But her eyes never left Jason. She was regarding him with a hostile glare.

"This is my brother, Jason," Brett explained. "Don't worry, he's cool."

"He hurt with little spear!" Neri said, accusing, and she made a shooting motion with her hands.

Jason realized she was talking about the crossbow and the whale. It took both boys several minutes to try to explain that the dart would do no harm and was only meant to help them learn more about the creatures.

Besides, Brett pointed out, didn't Jason come to

the aid of her and the turtle? Would he have done that if he meant them any harm?

Neri considered this and then seemed to relax a little.

Tentatively, Jason decided to bring up the subject of the island. He would like to see her home, he said. Would she take them there?

Neri thought a while before answering. "I ask friend," she said. "You be here when sun is again there." She pointed to the sky.

"The same time tomorrow?" Jason started to ask. But it was too late. With a flip of her body, Neri dived and was gone. They watched but she never broke the surface again in their sight.

"What did she mean about asking a friend?" Jason asked Brett. "I thought you said she was on her own?"

Brett looked blank and shrugged.

✳   ✳

Dianne was in a thoughtful mood back in their cabin that evening. She explained that she and Winston had been having some problems in the lab. The recordings of the whale singing were fine, and she was building up a big library of tapes. The trouble was with the screen.

Often when the blip showing their whale appeared, they would see another smaller one moving beside it. They had thought this was just a minor fault in the equipment. But now they were beginning to wonder if it wasn't another creature.

A porpoise, perhaps. Or a seal. It was just rather strange, she said. Still, she conceded, dismissing the matter, there were a lot of strange things in the sea.

Behind her back, Jason and Brett exchanged a look.

✳   ✳

"I should've known she wouldn't turn up," Jason said, disappointed.

He and Brett had been waiting out at the drift net site for two hours.

"Now who knows how long it'll be before we see her again!"

He was about to restart the engine when Brett gave a shout.

Neri rose from the sea like a porpoise, in one exuberant leap that carried her clear of the surface. For a moment, she hung in the air, flying free against the clear blue sky, before plunging back into the foam and bobbing to the surface.

"Friend says yes," she called. "You follow."

Even with the engine at full throttle, the boat could not match Neri's speed through the water, and she had to keep stopping to allow them to catch up.

As the water became shallower she guided them safely through a gap in the surrounding reef and into the calm seas that lapped against her island. They stepped ashore and Jason stared about in wonderment.

Snow white sands curved out of sight on either side. Beyond the beach, great stands of rainforest trees grew thick and tall, their trunks interlaced with vines and creepers. Brilliantly colored birds flashed from branch to branch and butterflies the size of bread-and-butter plates flitted through the air.

They made their way inland, Neri leading the way. Each turn of the track revealed new sights. Dripping clusters of bright tropical flowers. Little marsupials who sat up on their hind legs like tiny kangaroos and watched them pass. Huge emerald green frogs with golden eyes. With a whoop, Brett darted forward to try to trap one in his hands, but Neri caught his arm.

"No further," she said, indicating a tree just ahead with a mark blazed on its trunk. Then she pointed beyond and said, "Badlands."

"Badlands?" Jason queried.

"Don't go," she replied solemnly. "Bad things happen there." Without another word she turned on her heel and led them away down a sidetrack.

Later, as they frolicked in the cool waters of a stream near Neri's home, Brett fell to thinking about the frogs again. He'd never seen anything like them before. And one would make the coolest pet to show off to his friends on *ORCA*.

Neri and Jason were occupied, swinging out on vines above the stream and plunging down, he with a great splash, she with a knifelike entry that scarcely caused a ripple on the surface. Brett slipped quietly away. As he passed the marked tree, Brett could see several of the frogs hopping away down the track ahead. He hurried after them.

Jason and Neri didn't even realize he was gone until they heard his faint screams for help drifting on the wind. Neri was instantly on her feet and running. Jason pelted along behind, trying to keep up with her.

She hesitated for a moment when she came to the blazed tree, but Brett's calls, closer now, seemed to help her overcome her reluctance. She ran on down the track with Jason at her heels.

The country around them seemed to change almost immediately. Lush rainforest gave way to mangrove swamp, a world of twisted, stunted trees and acrid-smelling pools of mud and brackish water. They found Brett up to his neck in a particularly foul pond of thick, oozing slime. Having got trapped, he had tried to struggle out, only to bury himself ever deeper. Within a few more minutes, the clammy mud would suck him completely under.

Neri threw herself face down on the mud and kicked at Jason. It took him a moment to realize that she wanted him to hold her foot. When he had a firm grip around one slender ankle, Neri edged out, spreading her weight, and reached for Brett.

43

He managed to disentangle one hand and extend it toward her. Their fingers brushed. Once, twice. The third time, Neri lunged and grasped him around the wrist. Then she started to pull, slowly but steadily.

At first nothing happened. Then, with a reluctant slurping sound, the mud began to release its grip. As Brett came free, Neri looped an arm around his chest and dragged him back onto solid ground, where he lay gasping.

When he had got his breath back, he began to give his solemn word that he would never ever venture into the Badlands again.

Then he noticed that his brother wasn't listening. Jason was staring at something that lay amongst the mangroves at the edge of the sea nearby. Several rotting metal ribs jutted up in a line. Others fell askew at odd angles or had already broken loose from the spine of the structure and disappeared under the water. Incomplete as it was, Jason had no doubt what he was looking at.

It was the remains of a craft.

✳   ✳

"Is that how you came here? In that boat?" Jason asked. They were back at the place Neri called home. Having washed off the mud and dried himself by the fire, Brett was up a tree, examining the nestlike structure high in the branches where Neri said she slept.

Neri frowned at the question, as though not quite sure of the answer.

"Well, it looks like it was a decent size," Jason pointed out. "So there must have been a few of you."

Neri looked thoughtful, as if she was trying to remember something a long way back. "Yes, I think, Ja-son," she finally said, "when I am very little, perhaps many others. But all go. Soon only me and Father left."

"Father?" Jason said, surprised. "Well where is he?"

"Gone."

"Gone where?"

"Just gone—forever," she added simply.

"Jace," Brett called down, awkwardly, "I think she means he's, you know, dead."

"Oh," Jason said. "Sorry." But he noted that she didn't show any sign of sorrow at all. She simply acted as if it was the most natural thing in the world.

This unnerved him a little, but Brett chimed in. "Well, what about this other guy, this friend of yours? Who's he?"

"Jali," Neri said brightly.

Jason wasn't sure he'd heard it right. "Charley?" he queried.

Neri considered a moment. Her father had taught her to speak, but it had been many years since she had had reason to use words. Perhaps she had got it wrong. She shrugged. "Yes, Charley," she agreed.

"Does he sleep up here too?" Brett asked.

Neri threw back her head and roared with laughter. The two boys looked at each other in confusion as she shook her head and kept repeating to herself in disbelief, "Charley! Sleep up in nest!"

"What's the big joke?" Jason asked. "And whereabouts is this Charley anyway?"

Neri cocked her head to one side as though listening for something. Then she grinned.

"Just home," she said. "Come see."

She led them down to a sheltered cove. Jason peered around. There was nobody in sight. He was about to say something when he realized that Neri was intent, humming some strange tune to herself under her breath. Then she broke off, pointed out to sea and said, "There."

At that moment, Jason suddenly became aware that something was moving under the surface at the mouth of the bay, a large dark shape.

The creature breached, lifting out of the sea before coming down with a crash and a spout of water from his blowhole. Even at the distance, Jason could see that it was a fully grown humpback whale.

"Friend Charley," Neri smiled. She held up one arm in greeting. The whale slid under the surface. A moment later, his giant tail lifted into the air and the flukes swayed up and down in response.

Jason and Brett simply stood watching, dumbfounded, as Neri plunged into the water and headed toward him.

✳   ✳

"Did you believe the way she just swam out there and right up to that thing?" Brett whispered. They were back in their cabin on *ORCA* and they didn't want Mom overhearing anything.

Jason didn't bother answering. There didn't seem to be any point. They'd seen it with their own eyes. Neri's friend was a humpback whale. It was crazy but it was true.

They both lay in reflective silence on their bunks for a while. Jason finally spoke. "I tell you how I figure it," he said. "Wherever she came from, she was with a group of people on that boat. They must've run aground where we saw the wreckage, and couldn't get off the island."

"How old do you reckon she was?" Brett interjected.

"Hard to guess. She doesn't seem to understand time very well. But pretty young, I'd say. Anyway," he went on, "the rest of 'em died off pretty fast. Maybe they ate those berries, like you did, I dunno. But there was just her and her dad left. And then only her. So, with no one else around, somehow she made friends with Charley."

"Yeah, maybe, but how did she learn to swim like she does? I mean, you've seen her, Jace. She rockets along. And she stays down there forever!"

"I dunno," Jason replied, "but I reckon now we know what that little blip is Mom keeps getting on her screen."

There was a long, thoughtful pause before he went on quietly. "Listen, Brett, I don't think we should tell anyone else about her just yet. For one thing, I'm not sure she wants to be rescued. She seems really happy to me. For another, well, to tell you the truth, I kind've like having the island to ourselves. For a little while longer, at least. So we keep our traps shut and enjoy it while it lasts. Is it a deal?"

His hand appeared from the top bunk. Brett gave it a slap of agreement with his palm. "Deal," he said.

CHAPTER SIX

CHARLEY

Once they had discovered the way to Neri's island, Jason and Brett took every opportunity they could to slip away from *ORCA* and spend time there. This meant inventing imaginary fishing expeditions or other official *ORCA* duties that allowed them access to a boat. In this, they were aided by Brett's friend Froggy.

Froggy had a way with computers. He lived, breathed, and loved them. And above all others, he adored HELEN, the giant brain responsible for the day-to-day functioning of the *ORCA* complex.

Froggy's fascination with HELEN was well known. Commander Lucas had banned him from the bridge for tinkering with her. Even so, Lucas had, on occasions, been forced to come to Froggy when some technical hitch had defeated his own experts. He knew Froggy would come up with an answer. What he didn't know was that Froggy had discovered how to tap into HELEN from the terminal in the Lyceum after school hours. He would spend many a happy hour there after class fiddling and experimenting with her programs.

Froggy had one weakness other than HELEN and that was chocolate. For a Giant Whoopee Bar he would have been prepared to instruct HELEN to release the entire *ORCA* fleet to Jason and Brett. So he was only too happy to get her to officially issue them a single boat. He never even asked what they wanted it for. As far as he was concerned, it was enough to prove that he could do it—and the Whoopee Bar was a bonus. So, with transport made easily available, Jason and Brett were free to travel whenever their onboard duties allowed.

They liked to get an early start. Even the speedy ANT boats took an hour to get to the isolated island group, and they wanted to make the most of their time.

Only Vanessa ever seemed to question their comings and goings. One day she caught them by the main elevator just as they were about to leave and asked where they were disappearing to all the time. Brett muttered something about a fishing trip and they pushed past her. As she watched them vanish, Vanessa's beady eyes narrowed. Ever since the initiation incident she had determined that no one would ever catch her off guard again. So she was always ready to smell any hint of trouble. And, right now, the smell of it was thick in her nostrils.

✳   ✳

Time passed at a different pace on Neri's island, Jason noticed. One hour just seemed to drift into the next, with never any shortage of things to do.

In the morning, they would swing out on vines over the stream, ride the natural mudslides on its banks, or go exploring the hidden nooks and crannies of the rainforest. Then Neri would announce it was time to eat and head for the inlet they had dubbed Charley's Cove, since that was where he would be found, wallowing near the mouth, if he was at home.

There Neri would plunge in and gather fish. The boys had been astonished the first time they saw how she did this. When she was after larger prey, she would carry a barbed spear she had fashioned herself. But mostly, she went for the small sweet fish that flitted in giant schools through the reef. These she simply caught with lightning fast movements of her bare hands as she swam amongst them.

When she had gathered enough, Neri would lead the way back to her nesting tree. While the boys cleaned the catch, using sharp-edged shells, she would squat by the little circle of stones nearby. Using two rubbing sticks and a tinder of dried grass, she would soon have a fire crackling merrily away. Then they feasted on grilled fish, along with the nuts and berries Neri gathered from the surrounding forest.

Afterward they would sit around the embers of the campfire talking. As Neri spent more time with the boys, her speech improved. She still left words out from time to time, but she was less hesitant and stilted. She began to revel in this newfound ability by asking endless questions of them.

"Where your father?" she inquired out of the blue one day.

Jason flinched, "He . . . he doesn't live with us at the moment," he replied awkwardly.

"They're going to be getting a divorce," Brett piped in.

"They're just separated," Jason corrected him with an edge in his voice. "Dad said there were some things they had to work out and it was best we stayed with our mother."

Neri's eyes glittered excitedly. "You have mother?" she asked.

"Of course," Brett said with a snort. "You reckon we were found under a cabbage or something?"

"I not remember mine," Neri said reflectively. Then she turned again to Jason, eagerly.

"Tell me of her. Is she beautiful?"

Jason's face screwed up. He'd never really thought about Mom in that way. "Yeah, I guess so," he said finally. "But she's not much of a one for dressing up and stuff. She's too caught up in her work for that most of the time."

"That's a fact," Brett agreed. "It's always work first with Mom. That's the whole reason she volunteered for *ORCA*."

Neri pondered for a moment. "One day maybe I like to meet mother," she said quietly.

"I don't think that'd be a really good idea, Neri," Jason hastened to say, "at least not for a while yet."

But there was something in Neri's tone, a hint of determination, that made him feel suddenly nervous. He was very glad when she changed the subject. "I feel dry," she said, passing one hand over her brow.

It was yet another odd thing the boys had noticed about Neri. If she was out of water for more than a few hours, she seemed to weaken and grow pale. However, a quick dip in ocean or stream revived her almost instantly.

"Swim," she said, jumping to her feet.

As usual, they headed back to Charley's Cove after eating. Not to hunt this time, but simply to frolic in the sparkling blue sea. If Charley was around, Neri would often dive in and emerge out to sea alongside him. There they would sport together, Neri playfully leaping from the water in front of his nose or swimming circles around him to tickle his belly as she passed. In the meantime, Jason and Brett would content themselves with bodysurfing between the shallows of the reef or simply lazing in the sun.

However, this afternoon was different. Charley was there, but Neri just waved from the beach. Then she took Jason's hand and began to lead him out toward deeper water. "Come," she said.

"Where?" Jason sounded unsure.

"I show you Charley's world."

The tug on his hand was insistent. Jason just had time to suck in a lungful of air before he found himself underwater, being towed along in her powerful grip.

It was not until his lungs were nearly bursting that he managed to tear his hand free and kick for the surface. As he trod water, spluttering, Neri appeared, frowning at him. Jason had to explain that he could not hold his breath the way she could. A minute or two at the most, he told her.

This information seemed to amaze Neri. However, she agreed that Jason would squeeze her hand when he was running out of air and she would release him. It took a little practice. At first, Neri had a habit of taking him down again before he had properly caught his breath. But soon enough, they got it right and Jason found himself comfortably zooming along hand in hand with her under the sea.

For the next hour they soared through giant canyons of coral, flashed past sleepy-eyed turtles, and sent brilliant clouds of multihued fish skittering at their approach. Each time he came up for air, Jason could hardly wait to fill his lungs so that he could dive again. With Neri as his guide, it was like flying over a fantastic landscape of ever-changing shapes and colors.

Suddenly he became aware of something moving alongside them. He looked over. Charley was a little distance off, matching their pace with idle waves of his tail. From above the water, his size had been impressive. From underneath, it was staggering. And yet the huge creature escorted them along like a placid dog at heel.

Later, as he sat on the beach watching Brett take his turn to swim with Neri, a smile started to creep over Jason's face. To think he hadn't wanted to come to *ORCA* because he was convinced life out here would be too boring. And he had just been exploring the bottom of the sea with a girl and a humpback whale as companions! He lay back on the sand and laughed until his sides hurt.

✳   ✳

Vanessa was waiting on the *ORCA* pontoon when they returned late that afternoon. As they clambered up the ladder, she looked down into their boat and sniffed.

"I thought you went fishing?" she said, suspiciously.

"We did," Jason replied.

"Then where are the fish, eh?" Vanessa pointed to the empty creel in Jason's hand.

"So, we had a bad day, they weren't biting." Brett hurried in, adding, "Not that it's any of your business, Big Nose."

But Vanessa was not going to leave it at that.

"Well, I'm making it my business, you little creep," she called as they headed for the elevator entrance, "because I think you two are up to something. And I'm going to find out what it is."

✳ ✳

On the next trip to Neri's island, Jason came alone. And, it seemed to Neri, he was strangely troubled.

He explained to her that the day before had been Brett's birthday. Egged on by his friends Zoe and Froggy, Brett had eaten a record-breaking seven slices of birthday cake. He was now confined to bed with a record-breaking stomachache.

"What is birthday?" Neri asked when he had finished. Jason tried to make her understand, but Neri simply looked mystified. In the end, he gave up.

"It's not important," he said with a shrug, "not to Dad, anyway," and he walked away, biting his lip.

Jason was unusually quiet that morning, showing little interest in their usual pursuits. Instead he sat quietly by the river, lost in his own thoughts.

Finally, Neri came and sat in front of him. "You hurt inside, Jason. Why?" she asked.

Jason had not meant to tell her. In fact he had come to the island to try to forget what had happened. But suddenly, he found the whole story tumbling out.

He told her about Dad forgetting Brett's birthday, not even sending a present. How he had tried to contact Dad at his new place, only to have some strange woman answer the call. And how Mom confirmed that Dad had a new girlfriend and they were going ahead with the divorce. Jason knew what it all meant. He could no longer hold out any hope. Dad was never coming home.

Then, to Jason's shame, he heard his own voice break and felt tears stinging his eyes. He tried to turn away, but Neri put a hand on his shoulder, stopping him. She leaned forward, reached out and plucked a tear from his cheek with the tip of her finger. She stared at it, fascinated and confused.

"What is this?" she said.

Jason realized that he had never seen Neri cry. Not even when she talked about losing her father. Regaining control and wiping his eyes with the back of his hand, he asked her about it. Didn't she ever feel sad about him not being around anymore?

Neri shrugged, but her voice was steady. "Things go. New things come. That is the way of it all."

She touched his hand lightly.

Somehow, sitting there alone with her, Jason felt that perhaps she was right. That the pain he was feeling would pass in time and be replaced by other things. It was as though she had already started to lift a weight from his heart and he felt glad that, of all people, he had talked to her.

But the realization that Neri would not—or could not—cry had caught him by surprise. It was not to be the last surprise that day.

Later, as Neri was busy collecting fish for their lunch, Jason donned the mask, snorkel, and flippers he had brought with him and headed out into Charley's Cove. It was not as exciting as swimming with Neri, but still he felt a sense of peace coming over him as he drifted languidly through the coral, working his way into deeper water.

About halfway out, he surfaced and looked around. From a distance, he could see Charley basking out near the mouth of the cove. What he failed to see, as he submerged again, was a dark torpedolike shape moving in from the sea, drawn by the flapping of his flippers.

Neri was wading ashore when she heard the urgent call.

A fanged one is among us!

Then she saw the vision. The sleek, deadly form with its curved dorsal fin slipping past Charley as it honed in on its prey. She dropped the fish she was carrying and raced back into the water. With a series of mighty kicks, she began to streak out toward where she had last seen Jason.

He was just beginning his third descent to an

undersea grotto when Neri appeared from nowhere, grabbed him, and hauled him to the surface. "Out! Quick!" she yelled. The next thing Jason knew, he was being dragged through the water toward the beach.

"What the heck's going on?" he asked as he staggered up the sand.

"Shark! There is a shark!"

"What are you talking about, Neri?" Jason said, pointing out at the unbroken surface of the bay. "I don't see any . . . "

He froze in horror. At that moment, the fin of a great white shark broke the waterline right where he had been diving.

"But you were so far away," Jason said, when he finally found his voice again. "How did you know it was there?"

"Charley told me," Neri answered. And then she stopped, and her hand flew up to her mouth. Her father had warned her many times. Warned her that if she met Outsiders one day, there were things she should not tell them about her and Charley. They would not understand, he said. And now she had let the last secret slip.

Jason gaped. "Charley told you? How?"

Neri looked hard at Jason's face. He was not really an Outsider, she thought. Not anymore. And when he had shown her how water came from his eyes, surely he had shared his own secret.

"He sings to me," she said, "and I hear it in here."

She touched her forehead near the temple. "He tells me where he is and what he sees. And sometimes, when he hurts or fears, he sings very loud. Then I see, too, through his eyes."

"And you ...," Jason croaked, "can you sing back to him?"

"Of course."

Jason sat down hard on the sand, as if deflated. He put his head in his hands and was silent for some time. Then, finally, he gazed up at her intently. "I don't understand this," he said in puzzlement. "What are you?"

"I am Neri," she replied.

She walked down the beach and picked up the string of fish she had dropped. When she turned back, it was with a smile on her face. "Come," she said. "We go eat."

Afterward, as they sat around the campfire, Neri told him how it had begun.

She was only a little girl, she related, when one day she wandered away from her father and up onto the clifftops that flanked the cove. Venturing too close to the edge, she slipped and tumbled from the cliff into the sea below. She floundered for a moment, then began to sink like a stone.

Charley must have been in the bay and heard the splash to have arrived on the spot so soon. All she recalled was a great dark eye appearing beside her. Next thing, she was being lifted on his broad back up to the surface, where he nosed her into the safety of some rocks until her frantic father arrived.

He continued to haunt the cove and, by imitating his actions, Neri found she was soon able to travel safely through the water with ease.

"Then it was Charley who taught you how to swim the way you can?" Jason interrupted.

Neri nodded. It was in the course of these lessons, she went on, that she realized she understood him and they started speaking to each other. At the same time, their friendship was sealed forever. She fell silent.

"You didn't have to tell me all that, you know," Jason said quietly. "So why did you?"

"We are friends also, Jason," she replied, looking him in the eye. "Now I have seen what is in your heart, I know I trust you."

From that day on, Jason felt that a special bond existed between himself and Neri. When he headed back home that afternoon, she and Charley escorted him, cruising along in the wake of the boat. It was only when the *ORCA* platform came in sight that they heeded Jason's warning gestures and turned back.

※　　　※

In the laboratory, Dianne and Winston watched as the two blips on the screen swung around together. Nearby, the recorders hummed softly as they picked up the sound of the whale song issuing from the probe. Winston tapped at the smaller of the blips with a finger.

"There's his little friend again," he said. "And, listen, our chap's singing like a bird."

She nodded. "We've certainly got all our best recordings when that thing's with him. I wonder what the devil it is?"

"I recall an old Tibetan saying," Winston mused. "A wise man looks first for solutions in his own backyard."

"And just what is that supposed to mean?"

"That perhaps you already have the answer. In those boxes over there." He indicated the steadily growing pile of whale song recordings stacked in cartons on a shelf.

"You think there might be some clue on these as to what kind of animal we're seeing."

"Who can say?" Winston replied, "but it's worth a try isn't it?"

Without answering, she walked over to the boxes and began to take them down.

✳   ✳

"Neri can talk to Charley!" Brett was sitting up in his bunk, his stomachache forgotten in the excitement. Jason signaled him to keep his voice down.

"But how does she do it when she's swimming?" Brett went on in a whisper. "Wouldn't her mouth fill up with water?"

"It's not like ordinary talking, thickhead," Jason said. "It's more like with their minds. Some kind of telepathy."

"All the same, what's Mom gonna do when she finds out? She'll flip!"

"Mom's not going to do anything," Jason replied steadily, "because we're not going to tell her."

Brett scowled uncertainly. "We'll have to sometime, won't we, Jace? I mean, she is sitting up in that lab with a trillion dollars worth of equipment trying to figure out how to speak to whales. And Neri actually can!"

"Right. So what do you reckon's going to happen if we spill the beans? All those eggheads in lab coats would be taking Neri apart to see how she does it. There'd probably be bits of her in specimen jars all over the place before we knew it."

"Mom'd never let 'em do that."

"You know what she's like about her work. Besides, she mightn't have any say in the matter. You want to take the risk?"

Brett thought about it for a moment, then glumly shook his head.

"All right," Jason continued, "and if we can't tell Mom, we can't tell anyone else, either. Especially not your friends."

Brett objected. "My friends!" he said. "What about yours? Like Daggy and Jodie and that Lee you're always making goo-goo eyes at?"

"I do not make goo-goo eyes at Lee!" Jason said tautly, then added, "Anyway, most important of all, it's got to be kept from Vanessa. She's already sniffing around. If she ever found anything out, it'd be all over *ORCA* in ten minutes."

There was a little more discussion, much of which centered on the nature of goo-goo eyes and the fact that Lee was the commander's daughter, but in the end it was settled. Neither would breathe a word about Neri except to the other.

Satisfied at last, and tired from a long and eventful day, Jason rolled over and happily closed his eyes. But if he had known what was happening on the mainland at that very moment, his sleep would not have been so contented.

✳   ✳

The sign on the fence near the guardhouse appeared to say UBRI, but closer inspection revealed that it actually read UNDERWATER BIOLOGICAL RESEARCH INCORPORATED. And underneath was written the warning: AUTHORIZED PERSONNEL ONLY.

Beyond the fence a complex of white brick buildings was clustered on a rise overlooking a bay, and in the window of one of these, a light was still burning.

In that room, a tall thin man with silver hair was talking to a fellow in a lab coat. "I can't say I'm very happy with the way this project is progressing," the silver-haired man was saying. "Don't you people realize how important it is to the company's future?"

"Of course, Doctor Hellegren," the other replied, "but it is difficult to get results when your specimens keep disappearing. And humpback whales can be surprisingly elusive for such large creatures."

"Apparently not for our rivals on *ORCA*."

Hellegren picked up a file from his desk and waved it. "This is a report from a Dr. Bates in one of their marine biology labs," he said. "If it is to be believed, they have not only placed a tag on a specimen, they are making constant and clear recordings of his songs and brain patterns."

"But . . . how did you get that file?" the other man asked.

"At a good deal of expense, believe me. And not with their knowledge. The point is, they are already leaving us far behind. If there is a way to communicate with cetaceans, they are going to find it years before we do at this rate."

"Well, of course, if we had their facilities . . . "

"It is not their facilities we need, Johannson," Hellegren interrupted coolly, "it is their current research."

He threw the file down. "This information is already several weeks old. We must catch up with them and then keep pace."

"I don't see how that is possible."

"I do. I'm arranging for someone to work for us inside *ORCA*. They will make copies of Dr. Bates's recordings and smuggle them out. With high-speed equipment, it should not take too long for us to duplicate what they have to date. After that, it is simply a matter of sending us each day's results."

He leaned back in his chair with his hands behind his head. "And then, my friend, no one will discover anything about this whale without us learning about it at the same time." He grinned, showing teeth like a barracuda.

CHAPTER SEVEN

NERI'S WISH

"Honestly, Jason," Mom said, in bemusement, "sometimes I wonder what to make of you."

She handed back the certification that he had completed his final level of the scuba training course and was entitled to use *ORCA* equipment.

"When you first came here, it was all whine and moan about how much you hated it. Now you're getting boat licenses, diving licenses. . . . What's led to the change of attitude?"

"Hey, I'm just trying to make the best of it, like you said," Jason responded defensively. "It's no big deal."

"Well, Winston and I may be able to make use of another diver in the future," she grinned. "If all else fails, it might be our only chance of identifying that blip that travels with our whale."

Jason tried not to show any reaction.

"Still getting that, are you, Mom?" Brett asked innocently.

Mom nodded. "It really has us baffled," she said. "We've been going through all our recordings trying to get some clue to what it might be. But so far, nothing."

"Bad luck," Jason said as earnestly as possible.

"Oh, we haven't given up yet, believe me. Winston's got some other theory he's going to try out today. You can come and help, if you like, as long as you keep out of the way."

"Oh, that's all right, Mom. We're cool."

"No, I mean it. You're welcome. I hardly seem to see the pair of you these days."

"Thanks anyway, but we've sorta got things to do. Catch up with you tonight."

And before she could say any more, they were gone.

✳   ✳

They were well on the way to Neri's island when Brett noticed they were being followed. One glance through the ultrahigh-powered binoculars on board their boat confirmed their worst fears. It was Vanessa. She had been on the same scuba course as Jason and mentioned that she was getting her boat license as well. At the time, Jason had thought it was just her trying to prove that anything he could do, she could too. But now he realized she had other, more dangerous motives.

By this time, they knew the cluster of little coral atolls through which they were traveling reasonably well. Jason switched from the automatic navigation system to manual control and opened the throttle. Before Vanessa realized what was happening and increased speed, they were already disappearing behind the nearest atoll. Some dodging and weaving through the maze of outcrops jutting from the sea, a quick double back, and they had given her the slip.

Once he was sure they had shaken her off, Jason reset the automatic controls and they continued their journey, but he was worried.

"We're going to have to be more careful from now on," he said grimly to Brett as he continued to scour the horizon behind with the binoculars, just in case. "Things are starting to get tricky."

❋   ❋

There were some worrying developments on the island too.

Over the past few weeks, Jason had notice a subtle change in Neri. At first, she had shown no real interest in anything outside her domain except for a fascination whenever Mom was mentioned. But lately, she had taken to questioning them at length about their lives on *ORCA*.

"What is this television I hear you talk of?" she was asking Brett today as they sat around the fire, munching the last of the yams raked from the embers.

"Television?" Brett answered, his mouth still full. "Well, it's like . . . a sort of box thing on the wall."

"What do you do with it?"

Brett shrugged. "Nothing much. You just look at it."

"Why?"

"Well, because there are things on it."

"What things?"

"All sorts. You might get a movie . . ."

"Mo-vie?" Neri looked perplexed.

" . . . or football maybe . . ."

"What's football?"

"It's a game. A whole lot of guys run around passing a ball to one another."

"Why?"

"I dunno. That's just the way it is."

"But how do they all get in the box?"

Jason could see Brett was starting to get exasperated.

"They're not actually in the box," Brett tried to explain slowly. "It's just a picture of them. It's all done with electricity."

"What is elec-tricity?" Neri leaned forward eagerly.

"It's not important, Neri," Jason broke in. "You don't need any of this stuff here. And you wouldn't find it very interesting, anyway."

Neri considered a moment. "I think maybe I would," she said, finally.

Jason felt an icy touch down his spine at her words.

* *

Vanessa was in a furious temper when she returned to *ORCA*. She sought Jodie out in the galley, and Jodie sat, teasing her hair in a mirror, as Vanessa outlined her suspicions and recounted what had happened earlier in the day.

"The thing is," Vanessa said, "whatever it is they're up to, they know I'm onto them. So they're not going to let anything slip when I'm around. But *you*–nobody even notices that you're there."

"Huh?" Jodie had a feeling she should feel insulted, but she wasn't sure why.

"All I want you to do is keep your eyes and ears open," Vanessa went on, "and if you find anything out, let me know."

"But that'd be like spying. I don't think I could do that, Vanessa."

"You will, though, Jodie. Otherwise, I might have to tell who's been stealing peroxide from the lab stores to bleach her hair."

Jodie looked rattled. "Please don't do that. My parents'd kill me!"

"Well, then, you help me and I'll help you. Okay?"

Jodie nodded dumbly.

* *

For most of the afternoon, Neri had continued to ply Jason and Brett with questions about *ORCA*. What were their sleeping nests like? Where did they gather food? How did their home look? Who

71

were their friends? What was an elevator?

Brett had happily tried to answer her questions, but they made Jason feel nervous. For once, as they set out for the return journey he was quite glad to be leaving the island.

As they pushed the little boat clear of the beach, Neri caught his arm. "Jason," she said solemnly, "I have decided. I wish to see your home with my own eyes."

Jason went pale. "You mean go to *ORCA*?" he stammered. "You have to be joking."

"I show you my world. . . ." She gestured to the island, then pointed out toward the sea. "I show you Charley's world. Now you will show me your world."

He shook his head. "Uh-uh, Neri. Not possible. No way."

He tried to sound firm, but as she stood on the beach, watching them go, he did not miss the look of stubborn insistence that still lingered on her face.

✳   ✳

When Mom came home from the lab that night, she was bubbling with excitement.

"You should have been there today, boys. We have stumbled onto something fantastic!"

Brett took off his Virtual Reality helmet and glove, his birthday present from Mom. He had just finished playing Android Hunter and been zapped at level six. "Hmm?"

"Sit down and I'll tell you all about it."

She waited until Brett had joined Jason at the tiny foldout table before she continued. "Well, we were running our recordings through a sound analyzer. Naturally, we've been concentrating on the noises our whale makes. But then Winston accidentally switched to a different frequency spectrum. And suddenly, we heard something we never heard before. The tag is picking up a second sound."

Jason stiffened. Something told him this was not going to be good news.

"It's very faint because it's coming from outside. But in between the whale singing, something else appears to be singing back. And we think we know what it is."

She leaned toward them, hardly able to keep the smile off her face. "You remember the funny little companion of the whale's we keep picking up on the screen?" she continued.

Jason and Brett didn't dare look at each other.

"Yeah, sure," Brett said, a note of strain in his voice. "We know . . . the thing you mean."

"Well, we've established our chap is just calling over a short distance. And it's the only creature constantly around him. So we figure that's what he must be talking to! Not some other whale in some other ocean!" Mom declared triumphantly.

The boys said nothing. Mom started to look a little irritable. "Don't you understand what it means? The two of them can *speak* to each other."

She waited for a reaction. Jason finally felt obligated to speak. "That's nice, Mom," he said warily.

"Nice!" Mom exploded. "Look, this is possibly a major breakthrough. It's proof that two different species can communicate. That could be the key to us starting to unlock this language. And all you can say is it's nice!"

Mom glared at him. "Honestly," she continued, tight-lipped. "You know, Jason, it wouldn't kill you boys to show a little bit of interest in my work for a change. It really wouldn't!"

She turned on her heel and walked angrily away toward her quarters, leaving Jason and Brett in unnerved silence.

❋   ❋

"One thing you have to say about Dr. Bates," Hellegren said, "is that she does excellent work."

The sound of whale songs echoed through the main laboratory at UBRI headquarters. At the same time, a screen flickered with the undulating patterns of brain waves.

"Marvelous," his companion agreed, "I've never seen anything quite this good before."

"And these are only the very earliest recordings, Johansson. Our *ORCA* contact is sending them to us in the order they were made. No doubt, they shall get even better as they go along."

"You are quite sure this is safe, Dr. Hellegren? If

we should be discovered taking someone else's research. . . ."

"Relax, man. They will never know."

"All the same," Johansson persisted, "I am not entirely happy about this."

Hellegren turned a cool eye in his direction. "Need I remind you what is at stake here? Whoever is first to break the language barrier with these creatures can control them one day."

"Yes, I know the military possibilities are enormous, but . . ."

"Even in peace time," Hellegren insisted, "we are looking at multimillion dollar potential. For such rewards, one must be prepared to bend the rules a little."

Johansson nodded, conceding. Hellegren turned back to the screen. "A most interesting specimen Dr. Bates seems to have found herself," he mused. "I think we are going to learn a lot from this fellow."

❋   ❋

"You could have sounded a bit more enthusiastic, just to keep her happy," Brett commented as the boys prepared for bed.

"What is there to be enthusiastic about?" Jason retorted. "This is shaping up as a disaster. Mom knows something's talking to Charley. How long before she tracks it down to Neri?"

"It'll be cool," Brett said in his annoying fashion. "There's no reason why she should ever find out."

"Don't forget, we've also got Vanessa on our tails," Jason reminded him.

"So, we'll just have to be more careful from now on when we go to the island."

"And then there's this crazy idea of Neri's about wanting to see *ORCA*. That really worries me."

"Ah, she'll soon forget about that."

"Well, you'd just better hope you're right," Jason muttered, his brow creasing, "because if you're not, we're going to be in trouble right up to our necks!"

✳   ✳

Brett was not to know that Neri, lying in her nest, was staring up at the stars and pondering all the wonders that lay within the Outsiders' home on the bottom of the sea. Wonders, she decided, that must be seen with her own eyes one day soon.

CHAPTER EIGHT
THE BIG SHAKE

"If I'd known about this, I never would have done the scuba course in the first place," Jason grumbled, pulling his bathing suit on.

Brett set his Virtual Reality helmet aside. Try as he might, he still couldn't defeat Zorgoman, The Master Android. "What's up?"

"I just found out I've got to do a dive this morning and guess who they've given me as a partner? Vanessa!"

"Gruesome."

"You said it."

"Just remember to watch what you say."

"Listen," Jason replied, "you're not telling me anything I don't already know." And he headed grimly out to the equipment stores to pick up his diving gear.

✳   ✳

At that moment Vanessa was in the galley trying to talk to Jodie. But Jodie's attention was elsewhere. She was gazing adoringly at a tall, good-looking guy chatting at a far table.

"Isn't he gorgeous?" Jodie sighed. "His name's Billy Neilson. He just came on as a cadet in the computer division."

Vanessa's lip curled. "Don't you ever think about anything except boys, clothes, and makeup?"

"What else is there?" Jodie replied innocently.

"Listen to me, Airhead, this is important." Vanessa's temper was starting to run short. "When we get back from this dive today, I want you to go to work on Jason Bates."

"How?"

"I don't care. you should know better than I do." She indicated the copy of *Groovy Girl* magazine in front of Jodie. HOW TO IMPRESS A GUY was written across the front cover.

"Just get him talking," Vanessa continued, "and find out what you can. Understand?"

"Yeah, all right," Jodie said vaguely. Her attention was already wandering back to the handsome boy. "I've heard he's seventeen," she mused. "Do you think that's too old? I wonder if he's invited anyone to the big Easter dance yet?"

Daggy was coming past with Lee. "If you're

looking for someone to take you, I will," he volunteered enthusiastically.

"Get a grip, Geoffries," Vanessa said with a sneer. "No girl in her right mind would go anywhere with an ugly dag like you."

Daggy looked stung. His face flushed. He opened his mouth as if to say something, then thought better of it. He turned on his heel and headed out.

"That was really rotten, Vanessa," Lee said. "Why do you always go around bad-mouthing people?"

"'Cause I'm not a little suck of a commander's daughter. Next question?"

"You know, you think you're so much better than everyone else here. But one day, you're going to find out you're wrong."

Vanessa ignored her. "I'm due on a dive. Don't forget what we were talking about," she said to Jodie as she stalked off.

Lee went in search of Daggy and found him in one of the empty storerooms in Epsilon module. He was sitting mournfully by himself.

"She's right, you know," he said when Lee sat down beside him. "I'm just a dag. Someone to have a good laugh at."

"That's not true," Lee said.

"Yeah, it is. I always have been. Even when I was in grade school. A bunch of the boys told me we were going to do a naked streak through the playground. When the time came, guess who was the only one without any clothes on?" He pointed to himself with a nod. "If I could just do one thing well, it wouldn't be so bad. But I'm hopeless at everything."

"Don't run yourself down. Just because some people think you're a dag now doesn't mean you're going to stay one for the rest of your life. There's plenty of time to change. And I bet you'll turn out a real winner."

He brightened. "Yeah. Some day, I'm going to make them all eat their words," he said.

But that day was to be a long way off.

＊　　　＊

Jason was one hundred fifty feet underwater when Neri appeared.

He had completed his own dive and was now acting as safety buddy as Vanessa began hers. He watched her below him as she started a slow descent. Suddenly he felt a hand on his shoulder. Since he and Vanessa were alone, Jason nearly jumped out of his wetsuit. He spun around to see Neri gesturing urgently to him.

Quickly looking down, he was relieved to see that Vanessa was moving still further away, unaware of what was happening above her. There would be a few minutes before she would start to ascend again. The diving boat hull was almost directly over them. Jason indicated the far side of it. If Vanessa did glance up, at least that would offer them a little shelter from her gaze.

They came up together beside the hull and Jason pulled the air feed from his mouth. "How did you find me here?"

"Charley sees you," Neri replied. Glancing past her, Jason could see the plume of the humpback's spout some distance off.

Neri did not bother to explain further. She took hold of his shoulder, agitated. "There is danger! Charley tells me. Soon it is coming. Big shake!"

"Shake?" Jason was perplexed.

"Shake!" She held her hands in front of her and trembled them violently. "Earth shake!"

"Earth sh . . . ?" and then Jason realized. "You mean *earthquake*!"

"Yes! Go! You must warn your people!"

✳   ✳

Neri ran up the beach on her island and paused to look back out to sea. Charley was already sheltering in the cove, but through him, she began to hear the sound. A low rumble, far off, beginning to build.

She hurried into the rainforest to a giant hollow tree, crawled inside the natural fortress, a high-domed cave of wood surrounding her, and sat on the ground. She knew *she* would be safe. For her friends on *ORCA*, she could only hope.

✳   ✳

"An earthquake, eh?" Lucas regarded Jason with a cold eye.

81

"Yes."

"I think he's gone off his head, Commander." Vanessa was standing in the background, looking at Jason balefully. "He came down and dragged me out of the water halfway through my dive because of this."

Lucas referred to his control panel. "HELEN, do we have any indication of seismic activity in the area?"

A moment's pause, then HELEN's robotic voice replied, "Our sensors indicate negative, Commander."

Lucas nodded, then turned back to Jason. "I suppose this is your idea of a joke, then, is it? A bit of a laugh?"

"No. I . . ."

Lucas cut him off, curtly. "Well, you're going to find out I don't have much of a sense of humor. Especially when it comes to smart-aleck kids who think they can make monkeys out of me and my crew."

He called over his shoulder. "HELEN, locate Dr. Bates and have her come to the bridge at once."

"Yes, Commander."

"I want your mother to be here for this," he said to Jason, "then, perhaps, she'll understand that it's high time all of you got a bit of discipline."

Dianne was just coming in the door when the first shock hit. The whole bridge seemed to tilt, swaying crazily. Equipment toppled and crashed to the floor. Cables broke, showering sparks. The air was filled with the groan of straining metal. Jason and Dianne grabbed a firmly anchored stanchion and held on for all they were worth.

"Emergency level ten . . . emergency level ten . . ." HELEN started to intone.

"What the devil happened to the early warning system?" Lucas shouted above the uproar.

"We must have had an equipment failure in the sensors, sir," a young officer yelled as he frantically punched buttons.

The second shock split the hull down in Epsilon module. Water began to pour in. Daggy and Lee, who were still down there talking, had to run for their lives. They reached the watertight bulkhead doors just as HELEN was closing them in response to the incoming water. Daggy froze in horror.

"Come on!" Lee screamed, pushing him in front of her. "We're going to get trapped down here!"

They dashed through the rapidly narrowing gap. A moment later, the doors clanged shut behind them.

"Jeez, that was lucky," Daggy said, pale-faced. "I nearly missed my chance to make 'em eat their words. I would've died a dag."

When the third shock hit all the lights in the galley went out. Brett, Froggy, and Zoe cowered together under a table. Froggy moaned in fear.

"Stop being such a wimp, will you?" Zoe demanded.

"I can't help it. I come from a long line of chickens. It's in my blood."

Zoe shook her head. Boys! What a bunch of wusses.

Then the emergency lighting cut in, flooding the room with an eerie red glow. At that point, the candy machine short-circuited and exploded, showering the galley with chocolate bars. At least it had the effect of putting a stop to Froggy's whining. It was replaced with steady slurping and chomping sounds, only punctuated now and then with an occasional whimper.

After the third shock, there were no more.

On the bridge, Lucas ignored Jason and Dianne as he called for a damage assessment from HELEN. He quickly studied the three-dimensional diagrams as they came up on the screen, barking orders at the same time. Maintenance teams were dispatched to various sectors, while a small army was organized to pump out and repair the fractured hull in Epsilon module.

When Lucas heard of Lee and Daggy's lucky escape, he sent for them. First he embraced his daughter, then he proceeded to give both of them a scathing dressing-down for having been in the restricted area in the first place. "You, of all people, should know better," he growled at Lee. "Any more infractions of the rules, young lady, and you'll be going back to shore and a boarding school. And, I might add, I think you should do something about the company you're keeping these days."

He glared at Daggy as he said it, but Jason had a feeling the remark included him, too. Only when the last of the repair gangs had been consigned did Lucas turn his attention to Jason again. He walked over and confronted him.

"Very well," he said quietly, "so you were right. Now, would you care to tell me how you knew?"

Jason froze. In his haste to sound the warning, he hadn't had time to think about this. His mind raced. "It was . . . the fish." He grasped at a straw.

"The fish?"

"Yes," Jason improvised. "When we were out there, diving, I noticed they were behaving funny. Sorta like they were spooked or something. And I remember Mom telling me once that sometimes that's what it could mean."

Lucas snorted in disbelief. "Do you seriously expect me to believe that some passing sardine told you?"

"Now just wait a minute, Commander," Dianne said, wading into the fray. As Jason had hoped, venturing into the area of her work brought an immediate response. "Jason happens to be right," she went on. "There are recorded examples all over the world of animal behavior seeming to pre- dict earthquakes. And I believe that marine life does have the same capability."

"If you'll pardon me, Doctor . . . rubbish."

"Really?" Mom's hackles were rising. "Then how else do you explain it?"

Lucas eyed Jason doubtfully. "It was a fluke," he finally pronounced. "A coincidence. The boy just made a lucky guess."

As they walked away from the bridge, Dianne caught Jason's arm. "You always laughed at that idea, Jason. So how did you know?"

"I'm afraid he was right, Mom," he said, with a wry shrug. "I think it was just a lucky guess." And he walked away as fast as he could.

✳   ✳

The late afternoon sun was almost on the horizon when Neri emerged from the sea. She had spent a good deal of time with Charley, first checking that he was all right and then soothing him. Now that he was calmed and the danger had passed, her thoughts turned to Jason and Brett.

She stood for a moment looking out toward the west, to where she knew *ORCA* nestled on the ocean floor. For a moment, she looked undecided, then a little smile lit up her face. She dived back in and began to swim westward.

✳   ✳

The corridors of *ORCA* were almost empty that evening as most of the adults were occupied with tidying up their work areas and restoring damaged equipment.

Jason was making his way home from a game of simulo-tennis with Daggy in the recreation room. As he walked through a deserted viewing tunnel, Jodie hailed him. Jason frowned as she joined him. He was used to her always primping herself up, but this evening she looked as though she had made a special effort.

"Hi, Jodie. What do you want?"

She leaned her back against the transparent wall and pouted prettily. "I just thought we might talk. You know, we see each other around all the time, but we never really get a chance to speak alone, do we?"

"Ah, I guess not. Well, go ahead, shoot."

Jodie began to ramble on. Jason was quite perplexed. She seemed surprisingly interested in their fishing expeditions, even suggesting she might go along on one. He didn't know what to make of it. The idea of Jodie in a boatful of smelly fish just didn't add up, somehow. Then he saw something out of the corner of his eye that pushed everything else from his mind.

In the sea outside the viewing tunnel, right over Jodie's shoulder, Neri was approaching, waving to him.

She swam right up to the window and hovered there, smiling. If Jodie were just to turn around, there was no way she could miss her.

Then Jodie started to turn. Jason grabbed her by the shoulders and swung her back to face him.

"Well, listen, Jodie, I think that's a great idea," he said with all the enthusiasm he could muster. "Let's all take a boat out together one day and see what we can hook. . . ."

He managed to get one hand around behind Jodie's back, where she couldn't see it, frantically signaling to Neri to go upward, toward the surface.

"Just one rule, though, everyone's got to gut their own catch, right?"

Jodie's nose wrinkled. Behind Jodie, Neri saw the signal, nodded and, with one lazy kick, began to disappear from view.

"Eurrgh! Do I?" Jodie said with distaste.

"Yeah, that's the rule."

To his great relief, Neri's feet floated up and she was gone.

"Well," he said, "I supposed I'd better be heading on back to our cabin now. I've got things to do. But we'll definitely organize that fishing expedition some day, OK? See you."

He strolled on, rounded a bend in the corridor, paused for a moment, and looked back to make sure he wasn't being followed. Then he sprinted for the main elevator.

✳   ✳

Vanessa was waiting for Jodie in the galley. Around them, maintenance staff were still putting the finishing touches to the cleanup.

"Nothing happened at all," Jodie reported. "It

was really boring. All Jason did was talk about stupid fishing."

She sucked on the straw of her ProtoCola drink. "Vanessa, are you sure he's up to some funny business?"

"I'm sure, all right," Vanessa said quietly.

"Well, I've done my best. I'll still keep my ears open, like we agreed, but I tell you—I'm not putting my hands into any old fish guts for anybody."

✳   ✳

The elevator doors opened and Jason stepped out onto the platform. Avoiding the bright arc lights overhead, he picked his way from one shadow to another, scanning the whole area as he went. There was no one around. He went to the darkest corner and leaned over the edge. Below him, he could hear the waves lapping at the pylons. He called softly.

"Neri, Neri!"

Something broke the surface nearby and there was Neri's face looking up at him, grinning from ear to ear.

"What the heck do you think you're doing?"

"I come to be sure that you and Brett are safe."

"We're fine."

"And Mother?"

"Yeah, her, too. Now quickly, get out of here!"

But Neri didn't move. "Jason? How is it bright inside with no fire?"

89

"It's just lights, Neri. Nothing to interest you."

But to his horror, she reached out for the ladder and set her foot on the first rung.

"Now I am here, I wish to see."

"No!"

She paused.

"Neri," Jason continued desperately, "you can't come on board. It's too dangerous. I won't let you."

Even in the semidarkness he saw her eyes glitter.

"Jason, how will you stop me?" she asked, smiling.

Jason's heart sank because he knew he had no answer.

She climbed another rung.

"All right!" Jason called, halting her, "All right. I'll organize it. But not now."

"Soon." It was not a question but a demand.

"Yeah, soon as I can."

"Swear?"

"I promise. But please, just go before anyone sees you."

Neri dropped back into the water and her voice came out of the gloom. "Remember, Jason. You swear."

"I said so, didn't I? But right now, go back to the island. We'll come out and see you tomorrow."

She nodded then, with scarcely a ripple, slipped under the water and swam away.

Jason stared helplessly after her. Oh, no, he

thought. *What have I got us into now?*

※   ※

We're going to have to get her on board some-how," Jason shrugged. "There's no other choice."

Mom was still out, busy cleaning up the lab with Winston, so at least the boys could talk freely in their cabin.

Brett frowned. "Isn't that going to be awful risky?"

"It'll be even riskier if we don't. Now she's been out here once, there's nothing to stop her doing it again. And if she's floating around outside those windows, she's going to be spotted in no time. It was only luck she wasn't seen tonight."

"Well, isn't there some way we can put her off?"

"Don't you think I tried? But she's made her mind up. And, like she says, there's really no way we can stop her."

Jason began to pace, thinking aloud. "Here's the way I figure it. We smuggle her on just one time. Compared with the island, she's gotta find this place so boring, she'll never want to come back again. Then the problem's over."

"Hey, cool thinking. You're right."

"Let's hope so," Jason said grimly. "Otherwise we could be making the biggest mistake of our lives."

CHAPTER NINE
ON BOARD

"We're going to need a uniform and an ID card for her," Jason said quietly to Brett over breakfast.

"How long've we got?"

"About forty-eight hours. I told her to be here at dawn two days from now."

"You didn't give us much time."

"Listen, it was all I could do to make her hold off for that long."

"OK," Brett said, "but we'd better get moving pronto. You take care of the uniform. Leave the card to me. I've got an idea." A cheeky little grin spread across his face.

＊   ＊

"Fake an ID card?" Froggy said. "You've got to be joking."

"Hey, that's cool," Brett replied. "I knew you wouldn't be able to do it."

Froggy bristled. "I could do it standing on my head. But what would you want a false ID for?"

"I don't. It's just that some of the kids were saying you could do anything with a computer and I bet them that was one thing you couldn't."

"Well, you lose. It'd be a breeze."

Brett sucked in his breath and scowled thoughtfully.

"That's easy to say, Froggy, and personally, I wouldn't doubt you. All the same, I'd kind of like to see it for myself before I paid up."

"You're on. Meet me in the Lyceum after school's out and I'll prove it. Have you got any kind of computer cards?"

"Well, there's the games programs from my Reality Helmet."

"Perfect. But pick one you don't want anymore, 'cause once I change the bar code, that's it."

"No worries, Frog," Brett said happily. "I'll be there."

✳   ✳

Jason knew the right time to enter the laundry complex. All of the cleaning processes were automated. Soiled uniforms rolled in one side, were subjected to ultrasound washing, and came cleanly out onto racks at the far end. The only need for human input was to load and unload the racks. So at lunchtime, the staff all left for the galley and the place was deserted.

"Anyone here?" Jason called as he entered. He waited. As he had hoped, there was no reply, so he set about his task. He hurried to the racks of clean uniforms. Most were dark blue, though there were a few of the lighter shade that had only been issued recently. Jason walked along them, holding his hands up at what he judged to be Neri's height, looking for something approximately the right size.

For what seemed like ages nothing appeared to fit. If the height was right, the width was three times too big. If the shape seemed lean enough for Neri's slender body, the owner was apparently a midget. As he continued to search, Jason began to wonder if most of *ORCA* was staffed by mutations. Then he spotted one of the newer uniforms. It had a small tear in the coded owner's label at the back but it looked perfect for size. Jason took it from the rack and held it up against himself to judge, double-checking in a nearby mirror.

At that moment, a man with a delivery of soiled uniforms walked in the door. Jason froze. The man looked at Jason, apparently trying on one of the girl's uniforms, raised his eyebrows, and walked back out without comment.

Jason went scarlet to the ears. Then, tucking the

uniform under his arm, and grabbing a matching pair of shoes from the deodorizing machine, he hastily departed.

✳   ✳

Froggy punched a last sequence of buttons on the computer keyboard and spun around in his chair, holding the card out to Brett.

Brett examined it critically. "Are you telling me that HELEN'd actually accept this?"

Froggy smirked. "Not only that. She'd probably even say, 'Thank you, Mr. Duck.'"

"Who?"

"Well, I had to enter a name," Froggy explained, "so I used Donald Duck. Who cares? It's not like anyone's going to use it, are they?"

"Yeah, right," Brett agreed hurriedly.

"OK, so now for the final proof." Froggy took the card again, slipped it into a slot on the Lyceum master console, and tapped into the security sector. There was a momentary pause, then the words came up on the screen: SECURITY CLEAR-ANCE.

Froggy removed the card and waved it with a self-satisfied air. "There you are," he said, "easy as pie."

"Let's just have one last look at it," Brett asked.

"OK, but then put it in the disposal. I don't want anyone finding it."

Brett walked away with his back to Froggy. He had a piece of cardboard from the bottom of a chocolate bar ready, hidden in the palm of his hand. He put that into the disposal chute which whirred, shredding it. He slipped the ID card into his pocket.

"Thanks, Froggy," he said as he left. "You don't know how helpful you've been."

But Froggy was too occupied in wrestling with some new problem with HELEN to even bother answering.

❋   ❋

The light blue uniform and shoes lay on Jason's bunk.

"That better satisfy you, 'cause I'm not going back," he said. "I tell you, it was really embarrassing."

"You think you had the tough job?" Brett retorted. "Froggy's not easy to con, you know."

Then he grinned smugly, pulling the card from his pocket and flourishing it. "But I did it!"

Jason took the card and compared it to his own. "It's great," he declared. "You can't tell the difference."

"It's only a day pass, though," Brett pointed out, "so remember, whatever happens, she has to be off the base by 1800 hours. Otherwise, HELEN's going to start asking questions."

Jason found a spare holder, slipped the card into it, and attached it to the uniform. Everything looked perfect. When he looked up, he saw that Brett had a piece of paper in his hand.

"What's that?"

"Another one of my brilliant ideas. We want her to have a really bad time, right? So, I've made a list of all the most boring places we could take her."

He began to read. "Waste processing . . . the desalination plant . . . air-conditioning center . . . power plant control room . . ."

Jason peered over his shoulder at the list and chuckled. "She's going to wish she never came."

"Listen," Brett said confidently, "in ten minutes, she'll be begging to leave."

There was one thing left to do. They put the uniform and shoes in a couple of fishing creels and took them in the main elevator up to the platform. Once they were sure they weren't being observed, Jason led the way to one of the many large metal equipment boxes that were bolted to the structure at regular intervals.

"I've noticed no one ever seems to use this one," he said, "It's just full of old boat covers and things."

He opened the lid and stowed the clothes under a couple of layers of tarpaulin. "Well, that's it," he said as he closed the lid. "We're all set. Everything's under control."

※　　　※

In the laundry room Vanessa was stamping about in a fury. "Some moron's stolen my uniform!" she ranted.

"But Vanessa," Jodie said, meekly, "you've got it on."

"I don't mean this old thing, idiot. I just got one of the new issue ones. My father had to pull all sorts of strings to have me put at the top of the list."

"I've never noticed it on you."

"I hadn't even worn it yet! They say you should have it cleaned first to soften the fabric. And now, some cow's ripped it off!"

"Maybe it got mixed up with someone else's"

"Don't be stupid. It had my label in the back. There's only two possibilities. It's been stolen, or this is some sicko's idea of a practical joke." Her eyes narrowed. "Either way," she vowed, "somebody's going to be very sorry!"

✳   ✳

Jason and Brett were feeling pleased with themselves as they strolled into Mom's lab. They found the place a hive of activity. Crates were lying all over the floor and a youth was helping Winston to unpack and assemble a pile of strange-looking equipment.

"Hi, Winston," Brett said.

"Hello, boys. Oh," he added referring to the youth, "this is Billy Neilson from Computer Division."

Billy nodded toward them and went on with his work.

"What's all this?" Jason pointed to the equipment.

"This? It's an image synthesizer, of course."

"A what?"

"Image synthesizer," Dianne echoed, coming over from where she had been comparing whale song recordings. "It's all very experimental at the moment, but it's supposed to analyze sounds and construct a picture of what's making them."

"You mean, like if it heard the sound of a lion roaring, it'd come up with a picture of a lion?" Brett frowned.

"Well, it's not quite so exact, but that's the general idea."

"What are you going to use it for?" Jason asked, fearing he already knew the answer.

"Well, we've decided we'd like to find out more about our whale's little friend. We're hoping this might give us some clues. Maybe even enough to make a good guess what it is."

A few minutes later, Jason and Brett were heading for the galley.

"You don't think that thing could really work, do you?" Brett asked.

"I dunno," Jason replied. "She did say it was only experimental. Anyway, we've got enough to worry about as it is."

❋   ❋

The sun was just coming up two days later when Jason and Brett stood shivering on the platform, staring out to sea.

Brett spotted Charley first. He was a good way off, but even at that distance they could make out the great spout that went up from his blowhole as he surfaced.

"Jeez, you don't think she's bringing him with her, do you?" Brett asked in alarm. "We'd have fun trying to get him in the elevator!"

At that moment, Charley began to turn. He made a slow, graceful arc in the water then, with a flick of his tail, he dived again and was gone.

Neri broke the surface right at their feet. "Hello. I here," she said, with an excited grin.

"Just wait a moment," Jason muttered. He made a last check to see that nobody was around. "Okay. Up you come."

She scaled a ladder with ease and stood in front of them, dripping water. "Now you show me *ORCA*," she insisted.

"You can't go in looking like that. You'll have to change."

Jason led her to the equipment box and pulled out the uniform and shoes. "Quick. Put these on. We'll leave your own clothes in here and you can get them as you leave."

Neri nodded and started to pull her dress over her head. Jason's eyes popped, and Brett intervened hastily.

"Uh . . . it might be a good idea if you did that behind the equipment box."

Neri looked puzzled but went behind the box and swapped the clothes. When she emerged, she was wincing and frowning at the shoes on her feet.

"Must I wear these?" she asked. "They hurt." She squirmed in them uncomfortably.

"Yes," Jason said, adding hopefully, "unless, of course, you want to change your mind about doing this?"

Neri shook her head. With a sigh of resignation, Jason led the way toward the elevator. Neri clumped along behind, the unfamiliar shoes causing her to walk with a strange, stiff gait.

She looks like she's got a broomstick shoved down each trouser leg. Brett thought, as he brought up the rear.

"There seems to be an unauthorized person in the elevator," HELEN's voice said. "Please identify yourself."

Neri jumped, then peered around, looking for the source of the voice.

Jason crossed his fingers, took the ID card from her uniform, and held it on the sensor plate.

SECURITY CLEARANCE flashed across the screen.

"Thank you," Helen responded. "Welcome aboard *ORCA*, Mr. Duck."

"Whao!" Neri shouted in delighted alarm as the elevator hummed and started to descend.

✳   ✳

"That was fun. Can we go again?" Neri asked as the elevator doors opened at the bottom.

"No," Brett said.

"Come on," Jason took her by the arm. "Let's get this over with."

As they stepped out into the reception area Neri halted. Her jaw dropped and her eyes were wide as she stared about her at the bombardment of unfamiliar sights and sounds. Brett took her other arm and, flanking her, they propelled her toward the corridors. One or two passing people frowned at the sight of the girl with the odd walk, but they made it safely through reception and moved on into the heart of *ORCA*.

※　　　　　※

Dianne arrived at the lab to find Winston peering at a screen. He looked up at her approach. "Pity you weren't here fifteen minutes ago. You just missed something rather strange."

"Oh?"

"I switched the equipment on and suddenly there was the whale, right on our doorstep. Much closer than we've ever seen him venture before."

"Perhaps he's growing curious about us. Did you activate the recorders?"

"Of course. And he was singing. However, that was another odd thing. To my ears, it didn't sound like one of his inquisitive songs. It was more like those you have identified as him saying farewell."

Her brow furrowed and she began to move to the recorders.

"The wisest owl hears all before he flies," Winston quoted, stopping her.

She looked irritated. "Where on earth do you get these sayings from, Winston?"

"That was in a fortune cookie, actually," Winston confessed, "but I'm just trying to tell you I haven't finished yet. His little friend was with him."

"And?"

"The whale turned back, but the smaller blip kept moving toward us. In fact, it appeared to come right up to our front door, so to speak. And then it disappeared from the screen."

"You mean it's come inside the minimum range of our equipment?"

Winston nodded. "Which suggests it must be somewhere right on top of us."

"Well, don't just stand there, Winston," she said urgently, grabbing a pair of binoculars. "Let's go and see what it is!"

They spent the next hour up on the platform, scanning the surrounding water for any sign of life, but they saw nothing.

✳   ✳

Meanwhile, things had not gone quite as the boys had hoped. Far from being bored by the power plant, Neri was hypnotized. She gazed in wonder at the huge pipes through which water circulated with the motion of the tide to generate hydroelectricity. Finally, she pressed her ear gently against one pipe and listened. A smile came over her face.

"It's beautiful," she said in awe. "It sings like the sea."

Jason and Brett exchanged a concerned look

and quickly moved her on. To their dismay, however, Neri's interest and excitement only seemed to grow with each passing minute. In the air-conditioning center, she danced about in the constantly moving atmosphere, praising the warmth of the "winds." In the desalination plant she became fascinated by the low-slung lighting and kept trying to blow out the "little fires." At the waste-processing depot, she had to be dissuaded from diving into the huge tanks of steaming effluent undergoing treatment.

As they emerged into the corridor, Froggy and Zoe were approaching.

"Hi, guys," Froggy greeted them. "Coming up to the galley?"

"A bit early, isn't it?" Brett asked.

"Not for me. I'm starving."

Jason was aware of Zoe's questioning look at the strange girl beside them. Better to say nothing, he decided.

"We'll—er—catch you up there," he said, and Froggy and Zoe moved off.

"Why is he starving? There is no food?" Neri asked anxiously.

"Yeah, of course," Brett said. "It's just getting near lunchtime, that's all."

"Maybe time for you to leave, Neri," Jason suggested.

"No. Now, I wish to see where you live."

Jason's heart sank further. "You wouldn't like it.

It's really nothing interesting."

Neri turned her plea to Brett. "But I want to. I like to see where my friends live. I showed you my home," she pointed out and looked from one to the other in silent appeal.

Jason sighed and led the way.

✳   ✳

Neri stood in the cabin slowly rotating as she took it all in. "It's wonderful," she pronounced at last.

"Huh? You've got to be kidding," Jason said.

"Comfortable," Neri insisted. She peered into the shower stall, and frowned at the toilet. "But not this chair. This chair looks *not* comfortable."

"It's not a chair, exactly," Jason shifted uneasily.

"What is it?"

"Well, it's . . . um . . ."

Brett tried to assist. "You sit on it when . . . you . . . ah . . ."

Jason changed the subject by tapping a button on the control panel. "This is the shower," he said. Neri laughed with delight as the water began to cascade down.

"Inside rain!" she cried in disbelief. Then she was off in search of new wonders. "What is in there?"

"That's just Mom's quarters."

"Belongs to Mother? I must see." Before they could stop her, she was through the door.

She circled around the small table that held Mom's toiletries. "Pretty things," she muttered as

105

she examined them. Glancing up, she caught sight of her reflection. For a moment, she was startled, but then she smiled. "Is me. Like in a rock pool."

"It's called a mirror," explained Jason, but Neri wasn't listening. She picked up a small bottle from the table and examined it.

"Drink?" she asked.

"No, perfume. It smells nice. Women squirt it on themselves."

"How?"

Brett indicated the button on the top. Neri immediately pushed it, dousing him with perfume.

"Go easy," Jason said. "That's Mom's one big luxury."

As he took it from her, Neri spotted the framed photograph of the boys with Mom standing nearby. She peered closely at it. "Very good drawing. This is Mother?" She pointed.

"Yeah."

"Very beautiful," she said quietly.

"Look, come on, let's get out," Jason interrupted, "otherwise Mom's going to suspect that someone's been in here."

"Yes," Neri agreed, "I hungry now. You take me where the starving boy has gone."

"No, that's not a good idea."

Neri gave Jason a hurt look. "You will not share your food with me? I share all mine with you."

"You don't understand. It could be tricky."

"I understand," Neri said flatly. "You are shamed

for your friends to see me with you."

Jason groaned. This was becoming more complicated by the minute.

"Jace," Brett beckoned him aside and spoke quietly. "If she's gonna stay all day, we can't let her go without anything to eat."

"You want to let her loose with all those other kids around?"

"Hey, we've got away with it this far, haven't we? No one's really noticed anything. Get a table by ourselves and we could be in and out again before they're any the wiser."

It was against his better judgment, but the hurt look on Neri's face made Jason finally concede. "All right, we'll take you to the galley," he said reluctantly, "but you have to keep as quiet as possible. Let us do all the talking. You just agree with anything we say, all right?"

Neri nodded enthusiastically.

As they trooped out, Jason hissed in Brett's ear. "Just remember, this isn't my idea. I only hope we're not making a major mistake!"

INTO THE
LION'S DEN

I didn't think there were so many people in the world!"

Neri stood at the galley door, staring in. The lunchtime crowd of kids were milling around, punching orders into the electronic menus on the counter or waiting at the other end for them to materialize down the dispenser chute.

Jason and Brett guided her toward the counter. Lee was just finishing ordering as they came up.

"Oh, hello, Jason."

"Hi, Lee."

Neri echoed him with a big smile. "Hi, Lee!"

Lee looked a little nonplussed, but nodded to the stranger before heading off to the dispenser. Jason sounded a caution from the corner of his mouth.

"Don't talk. Just choose something to eat."

"That looks good," Neri said, pointing to a triple-decker hamburger going past.

"Er, Jace, why don't you grab a table and I'll do the ordering," Brett suggested, adding in an undertone, "I'll get her a plate of revegiton."

Revegiton was a thick green substance made from recycled vegetable matter and seaweed. It was cheap, highly nutritious and tasted like moldy old socks. Some parents insisted that the galley computer issue at least one serving a day to their kids, but it was almost always pushed aside. There was nothing guaranteed to cure an appetite as fast as a good big plate of revegiton.

Brett tapped in their credit code and ordered a double helping. They'd be out in no time, he thought, pleased with himself.

There was a disturbance in the next line. Two very large girls known as Valma and Valerie were pushing into the line in front of Zoe and Froggy.

"Hey, we were here first," Zoe protested.

"Buzz off, Shorty," was Valma's response, as she held her fist under Zoe's nose.

Zoe knew she stood no chance against the older girls. Disgusted, she turned to Froggy. "Thanks a lot for sticking up for me," she said, sourly.

"Hey, what could I do?" Froggy said in injured tones. "I couldn't hit a woman."

"You! You couldn't punch a train ticket," Zoe retorted.

Jason had located an empty table. Brett came over, bearing a large plate of green matter and set it in front of Neri. She sniffed it.

"Smells good," she said. She reached out, grabbed a handful and struck it in her mouth. "Tastes lovely!" she exclaimed and started to reach for another handful.

"No, Neri!" Jason hissed. "Use a spoon. Like this." He picked one up from the table and quietly demonstrated. Neri reached for her own spoon to follow suit.

Across the galley, Jodie, sitting with Vanessa, wrinkled up her nose in distaste. "Yuk! Did you see that? That girl was actually eating revegiton! And with her fingers!"

Vanessa looked around. "What girl?"

"The one over there with the Bates brothers. Who is she, anyway?"

Vanessa's eyes narrowed as she peered at the unfamiliar face. Then something else caught her eye—the uniform the girl was wearing. Vanessa's eyes grew narrower still.

"Mind if I sit down?" Jason jumped. Lee had come up behind him.

"Well—er—" he began.

"Yes. You sit down." Neri beamed.

"You're new, aren't you?" Lee asked as she sat.

"She's just started on the cleaning staff," Jason intervened hurriedly. "Part-time, so she's only on a day pass. Her English is still a bit rough because she's—Latvian," he added in an inspired after-thought.

"Oh. So Jason and Brett are showing you around?"

"They are my friends," Neri said, happily chewing.

Lee looked questioningly at Jason.

"We—we knew her before, you see," he explained.

"Back on land," Brett added. "You could've knocked us over with a feather when we saw her here."

"Where did you meet?"

"At school," Jason replied.

"On a holiday," Brett said at exactly the same time.

Jason chose the best of both worlds. "On a school holiday," he corrected himself.

They were interrupted as Froggy and Zoe joined them, unasked. A moment later, Daggy materialized, pulling a chair right up beside Neri and gazing at her with unabashed interest. Oh, no, Jason thought.

"Hello, I'm Damien," he said eagerly. "What's your name?"

"Neri," she said, scooping up the last of the green residue on her plate. At the same time, she toyed with the tomato sauce container in front of her with her free hand. She turned it upside down and watched with fascination as great glops of the red

111

mixture inside began to run out onto the table. Jason belatedly grabbed the container and pried it from her fingers.

"She's always been a real clown," he explained to the others with a forced laugh. But there was a harsh note in his voice as he added quietly, "Stop fooling around, Neri!"

In the meantime, Daggy's mind was working overtime. He was trying to think of something to say to this pretty new girl. Something that would impress her. He found it.

"Did you know that there's an animal called the bongo antelope that has a tongue so long it can stick it right up its own nostril?" he said. "It's true. When it wants to clean its nose it just . . ." And he proceeded to attempt to demonstrate. He was greeted with gagging noises and complaints of "Do you mind? I'm eating!" from the others. But Neri considered what he had said in grave silence.

"Interesting," she pronounced at last.

Daggy's heart soared. "Oh, I know lots of things like that," he told her. "Listen, I could tell you some more while I show you around, if you like."

"We're already doing that," Jason said firmly. "So, if you're finished, Neri . . ." He started to rise.

"No," Neri said, pushing her plate forward. "Still hungry. More of this, please."

Daggy scrambled eagerly to his feet, reaching for the plate. "Allow me."

But Brett beat him to it. "No, I'll get it."

In sudden close proximity to Brett, Daggy gave a sniff. His eyebrows raised at the whiff of Mom's perfume emanating from him.

"Hey, I like your perfume. Just gorgeous!"

"Get out of it, Dags," Brett countered, and gave him a light thump on the shoulder. Neri looked alarmed.

"Why do you hit him?" she asked.

"It's not serious. Just being friendly," Brett explained.

"Ah, you hit to be friendly," she mused, "I will remember that."

From the other end of the galley, Vanessa watched the goings-on at the far table with an eagle eye. "I think that's my uniform," she muttered.

Jodie looked up from her magazine. "What?"

"The one that girl's wearing. I could swear it's mine."

"But they all look the same."

"To you, maybe. But there's something about that one. . . ." She trailed off, then added accusingly, "Besides, I've never seen her before. She's new on board. Those uniforms were supposed to be issued to the long-timers first. So how come she's wearing one?"

"I dunno. Maybe her dad pulled strings like yours did. Anyhow, there's no point stewing about it. It's not like you could prove it or anything."

"Oh, yes I can," Vanessa's eyes were firmly

locked on the girl at the other side of the room. "And the moment I get the chance, I'm going to."

✳   ✳

"He's still circling, Dianne," Winston said, tapping the screen.

She came across and looked over his shoulder. The large blip was about a half mile away, tracing a steady orbit around them. The whale had been doing this without stop since he had reappeared on their equipment.

"There's no way this is random behavior," Winston said, checking his watch. "He's been at it for two hours now."

At the same time the lab was filled with the sounds of his singing. But there was something strange about the song this time, a plaintive, haunting note almost as if he were calling to someone.

"I don't understand," Winston said with a frown. "What's his sudden interest in *ORCA*?"

It was a question neither of them could answer.

✳   ✳

The rest of the kids had drifted off about their business and only Jason and Brett were left at the table with Neri as she finished her fourth plate of revegiton and sat back with a satisfied sigh.

"Had enough now?" Brett asked, incredulously.

Neri nodded.

"Then let's get out of here," Jason said, getting to his feet. They had, he thought, managed to steer a course through rocky waters only with a good deal of luck. Their friends had found Neri a little strange, perhaps, but they had successfully pulled off the charade. Nevertheless, he was keen now to get her away from public scrutiny and off *ORCA* as soon as possible.

They were out in the corridor heading for the elevators, when he realized they had company. Looking back, he saw Vanessa coming up behind them with Jodie trailing at her heels. Vanessa was watching Neri closely, as though sizing her up.

"Hang on, I want to talk to you," Vanessa called.

"Yeah, well, we don't want to talk to you," Brett replied as they continued on to the elevator well. Jason touched the call sensor on the panel.

"I want to know where she got that uniform," Vanessa demanded, as they waited.

Neri started to open her mouth but Jason quickly cut her off. "Like that's any of your business, Vanessa?"

"I happen to think it might be. You don't mind if I have a closer look?"

Jason moved to keep her at bay. "Yeah, she does as a matter of fact. What is your problem?"

"I want to see the code tag."

"What are you, the Clothes Police?"

"I'm the owner of a new uniform that's mysteriously disappeared. And it was exactly the same size as the one she's wearing."

Oh, no, Jason thought to himself. God, no—not

Vanessa's uniform. Behind him the elevator doors opened. He edged Neri into it. Vanessa moved to follow, but he and Brett stood firmly in front of the doors to prevent her. Vanessa confronted them.

"I tore the tag on mine getting it out of the wrapping. So let's have a look at that one."

Down on Delta level, young Billy Neilson, on his way to a routine service job, pushed the elevator call sensor.

"Buzz off, will you?" Brett chimed in. "It's not our fault if you go around losing your clothes."

Then they heard the soft click as the doors closed behind them. Jason made a desperate lunge for the control panel but the elevator was gone, bearing Neri away without them.

"Oh, no!" Jason cried. He and Brett exchanged a look of alarm, then raced for the next elevator.

At Delta level, Neri stepped out of the elevator and looked around her. She had not meant to become separated from the boys, but now she was, she thought it would give her a chance to look around without them always hurrying her on. She chose a direction at random and wandered off down the corridor.

Jason stopped the elevator at Beta level. Both heads popped out. There was no sign of her.

"She could've got off anywhere!" Jason said urgently. "You search here. I'll go down to the next level."

Brett jumped out and began to scour the maze of corridors. Down at the next level, Jason was doing the same.

Meanwhile Neri wandered aimlessly, taking in the marvels around her. She meandered along, occasionally stepping into an occupied elevator to change levels. It wasn't until she started to feel faint that she realized how time was passing. And fortunately, right at that moment, she saw a familiar face. Daggy was coming around a corner just ahead.

"Hey, Neri," he greeted her, the pleasure on his face obvious.

"Hello."

"So . . . what's happening?"

"I feel dry. You have water?"

"Sure. There's a cooler just down here." He led her to a drinking fountain. Neri looked at the strange device unsurely.

"Oh, let me," Daggy hurried to say. He turned the fountain on. Neri smiled with wonder at the jet of water arcing though the air. Then she put her head under it. She did not emerge until she was completely soaked.

"Better now. Thank you," she smiled to Daggy and continued on along the corridor. Daggy watched her go with his mouth open and a look of complete puzzlement on his face.

Further along, a stifled cry of protest caught Neri's attention. She looked. In an alcove, she saw

Zoe with her back to the wall. Advancing on her were the two large girls, Valma and Valerie.

"Hey, Zo Zo, you little shrimp. We've been looking for you," Valerie said with a smirk.

"Give me a break," Zoe protested.

"Sure. Which arm?" Valma said, reaching for her arm and twisting it. As Zoe tried to struggle free, she lashed out, hitting her tormentor on the shoulder.

"Get off my case!" Zoe complained.

Neri smiled. She remembered this from the galley. It was how people showed they were friends. She walked up to Valma. She would show that she was a friend, too.

"Get off my case!" she cried cheerfully and punched her in the shoulder. Valma shot across the alcove, hit the back wall at full speed, and losing her footing, slid to the floor. Valerie immediately dropped Zoe's arm and started to back warily away.

"You are friend, also?" Neri asked, approaching her with a fist already cocked. Valerie took to her heels and fled. Neri watched her go, confused.

"Wow! Stick around," Zoe said. "You can be my bodyguard any time."

"No, I must go now," Neri said, still bewildered. "I must see everything. Good-bye."

As Neri disappeared, Valma was still picking herself up off the floor.

Riding the elevator to the next level, Neri found

herself in a wider corridor with many doors leading off it. There were people in white coats in the rooms beyond and some looked at her questioningly as she passed. She began to feel she was not welcome here and was about to turn to leave when she heard something familiar.

It was Charley's song. And it was coming from the last room. She made her way toward it and looked in the open doorway. It was like a magical place, a cave filled with unknown objects that beeped and shone and gave off lights. And in the air, she could hear Charley's song clearly, too, calling to her. Irresistibly drawn, she entered. She began to answer Charley, humming reassurance softly under her breath.

Don't worry. I am well and I will return to you soon.

And then Neri realized that she was not alone. A man and a woman were at the back of the room, watching her curiously. The man she did not know, but the woman she recognized instantly. She began to come over.

"Hello, I'm Dianne Bates. Can I help you?"

It was Mother, and she was even more beautiful than in the good drawing.

"Are you new on *ORCA*?"

"Yes. Today."

"Ah, then you shouldn't be wandering about by yourself. You'll get lost. Or are you already?"

A voice interrupted from the doorway. "Young lady, do I know you?" Commander Lucas stepped in, looking Neri up and down. "Who is this girl, doctor?"

"She's new here. I think she's lost."

Lucas glared at her ID badge. "Day pass only. Must be a worker. Well, go back to Reception, call your supervisor, find out where you're assigned, and go there. Don't let me find you wandering around again."

He pointed the way and Neri fled. She rode up in the elevator again and found herself finally at a place she recognized, back at the galley. She peered in, looking for the boys. They weren't there, but Vanessa was, sitting with Jodie.

"Well, well," Vanessa said, "look who's here. Why don't you and I go and have a little chat?"

Neri looked uncertain. "I must find Jason and Brett," she said. "You have seen them?"

"Yes, I know where they are. In the recreation room. Come on, I'll show you the way." She took Neri's arm and led her off.

A minute later the elevator doors opened again and Jason and Brett emerged.

"Well, I searched everywhere," Brett said as they headed into the galley. "No sign of her."

"Me neither. It's like she's disappeared."

Jodie looked up as they entered. "What are you doing here?" she asked innocently. "Vanessa just said you were in the rec room. She's taken that girl there to find you."

"You don't mean Neri?" Jason stammered.

Jodie nodded.

The boys flew back out the door.

"Where are they?" Neri asked, looking around the empty room.

"They were here a minute ago," Vanessa lied. "Just wait, they'll turn up. So, they're old friends of yours, eh?"

"Yes." Neri was starting to feel a little nervous.

"Quite a coincidence. You look pretty young for a cleaner. How did you get the job on *ORCA*?"

"I must go now."

"Sure. Soon as you've told me where exactly you got that uniform." She began to circle around behind Neri.

"I must go," she repeated.

"Why?" Vanessa's hand reached for the back of the tunic. "Unless you have something to hide. . . ." She began to edge the neckband over. A half inch and she would be able to see the tag.

The boys burst through the door. Jason grabbed Neri and pulled her toward him. "Neri, we've been looking everywhere! Come on, time's wasting!" Jason said urgently.

"Not until you tell me what's going on!" Vanessa wailed. "That's my uniform!"

"You're a very confused person, Vanessa. It's not yours."

"Then let me see the tag!"

HELEN's voice suddenly floated through the air. "Your attention please. Would all day pass

121

holders report to Reception prior to departure from *ORCA*."

"That's you, Neri. Gotta go. Sorry, Vanessa. Right now."

"Yeah, right now," Brett echoed as they bundled her out the door.

They managed to get her up to the pontoon before the boat arrived to take the day staff back to shore. She hastily changed back into her dress behind the equipment box.

"It was a good day," she chirped, handing the uniform to Jason.

"You reckon?" he said flatly.

Neri pointed to the equipment box. "You will hide it there? For when I come again?"

"Again!"

Brett was pointing, agitatedly. "Jace, the boat's coming in!"

"All right, I'll hide it! Just go!"

"See you soon," Neri said in farewell. She slipped off the platform and disappeared under the water.

Jason looked at Brett, exhausted. "She wouldn't really come back, would she?"

"What do you reckon?"

Jason met his little brother's steady gaze. Then he put his head in his hands. "Oh, my God," he moaned. "What have we started?"

CHAPTER ELEVEN
RAPTURE OF THE DEEP

Only a few days had passed since Neri's first, chaotic visit to *ORCA* when she begin to hint she would like to return. There were so many things, she said, that she wanted to see again.

Jason tried to talk her out of it, but he knew in his heart that his efforts were doomed. So a deal was struck. She could come one more time, they agreed, but only when the boys said so. "There's something important we have to arrange first," Jason said.

They took Vanessa's uniform from the equipment box where it lay concealed and pulled out the incriminating code tag, which they flung into the sea. Then they replaced it with a new tag, one of Mom's. It was off a jacket she rarely wore and if she noticed it was missing, she didn't mention it.

The day Neri came back on board, Vanessa made a beeline for them the moment they entered the galley. When she again laid claim to the uniform, Jason shrugged and suggested she check it. Vanessa immediately looked at the back of the tunic. Her face fell. It was obvious at a glance that the bar code was not hers. As she walked away, frowning, the boys and Neri shared a secret grin of triumph.

When Vanessa rejoined Jodie at their table, her frown had turned into a scowl and her eyes were hard with suspicion. "I still say they're up to something weird," she muttered to Jodie. "And I think whatever it is, that girl's involved in it, too."

The rest of Neri's second visit went surprisingly smooth. Daggy followed her with adoring eyes but their other friends simply greeted her as they would any new acquaintance. Jason had spent some time coaching Neri on her new identity and the others seemed to accept it without question. Neri stayed close to the boys and, apart from her rather peculiar way of walking in the unaccustomed shoes, she did little to draw attention to herself.

Jason and Brett were feeling pleasantly relieved as they walked Neri toward the main elevator on her way out, then Mom spotted them across the other side of the reception area. She was having a heated discussion with Commander Lucas. They seemed to argue a lot, mostly about lab equipment that she said was necessary and he refused to authorize, saying it was a waste of money. She was in the middle of a sentence when she glanced over his shoulder and saw them passing, laughing together.

Jason, realizing they were being watched, quickly led the way to the elevator and opened the doors. A moment later, they were speeding upward.

"This'll have to be the last visit for a while," he said to Neri as she changed into her own clothes behind the equipment box. "We can't risk it too many times. You've seen just about all there is to see, anyway. So you stay away and we'll come out to the island whenever we can. All right?"

Neri nodded reluctantly, and insisted on seeing the uniform placed back in its hiding place from where it could be retrieved. Then she plunged off the platform, waved, and slid beneath the surface.

"Who was that girl I saw you with today?" Mom asked, back in their cabin that night.

"You mean Neri?" Brett said, without thinking.

"She's just a friend of ours," Jason added carefully.

"You looked like old pals from way back, I must say," Mom lifted an eyebrow. "She's a strange little thing, though."

Jason gulped, but said nothing.

"She wandered into the lab the other day." Mom

went on, "She was humming along with the whale song as though it was some tune she knew. And she has the most unusual eyes."

"Yeah, you could say Neri's a bit different, I guess," Brett agreed with caution, "but that's what we like about her."

"It's an odd name, too, Neri. Do her people have anything to do with the sea?"

Jason could feel his throat tightening even further. "I don't know. Why?"

"Well, in the old Greek myths the Nereids were sea nymphs. Rather like, well, mermaids, I suppose you could say. I just wondered if that was where they got the name from."

Brett forced a laugh. "Yeah, sure, Mom. Me and Jace spend a lot of time hanging out with mermaids. And next week, we're playing simulo-tennis with the Loch Ness Monster. Ow!"

Mom connected with one of her friendly cuffs then followed it up with a hug. "Smart aleck," she grinned, and walked away, smiling.

Later, the boys lay in their bunks, whispering in the dark.

"You don't suppose there's any chance that she actually could be one?" Brett asked. "A mermaid, I mean?"

"Get a grip," Jason hissed back. "There's no such thing. She might be different but she's not that different. Besides, we know where she came from—that wreckage in the Badlands. She'd hardly have needed a boat if she were a mermaid, would she?"

"No, I guess not. And I suppose she'd have to have a tail, too."

"Mind you, I reckon Mom'd think she was the next best thing if she ever discovered the truth. That's why we've got to make sure she never even sees Neri again."

✳   ✳

Mom's face seemed flushed with excitement as it appeared on the communicator screen. "Come up to the lab, boys. There's something you might want to watch."

When they got there, Winston and Billy Neilson were connecting up the last of the synthesizer equipment while mom watched. The boys nodded to Billy.

"That's about it, Dr. Seth," Billy said. "Want me to hang around in case I'm needed?"

"No, thank you," Mom said. "We'll take care of everything from here."

Billy looked a little disappointed as he left, Jason noted to himself. But he shrugged it off and joined the others at the main screen. On it the two blips could be seen clearly, moving side by side through the ocean. The sound of whale song crackled through the loudspeakers.

Under Dianne's direction, Winston narrowed down the computer's coordinates to concentrate on the larger blip.

"Right. Now, try patching in the Image

127

Synthesizer." Dianne's eyes were narrowed in concentration as she peered at a second screen sitting to one side of the bench.

"If this works, the program will identify the object and throw it up on here," she muttered absently to the boys.

For a short while nothing happened, then a shape began to form. It solidified into a recognizable image, the vast body and huge flukes unmistakable.

Jason felt Mom grip his arm with anticipation.

"You see? That's the whale. It's doing it!" she said, then added, "All right, Winston, now for the real test."

Winston fiddled the coordinates to center on the smaller object. At the same time the whale song faded, to be replaced by another sound, a faint, intermittent call like some far-off voice humming out a tune.

Again, after a pause, something began to take shape on the screen. Dianne's jaw began to drop as the body and head became clear. Then the arms and legs.

"That's like no sea animal I've ever seen before." Her voice was a puzzled whisper. "It looks almost . . . human."

There was a long pause while she and Winston gazed at it. Finally she turned to Jason, her brow deeply furrowed.

"Do you remember when we went out to tag

that whale and you claimed you saw a girl in the water?"

Jason laughed as convincingly as he could.

"Oh, come on, Mom, you don't think I really . . ." He shook his head, and pointed to the equipment. "This thing doesn't work properly, that's all. I was only trying to get us thrown off *ORCA*. I made the whole thing up."

✳   ✳

"She had to believe me, of course, but all the same, be careful, Neri."

The boys and Neri were sitting together around the ashes of the campfire on the island the next day.

"Maybe you'd better try not to go swimming with Charley quite so much," Jason said.

"Not go swimming with Charley?" Neri looked at Jason as if he was mad, and he knew immediately that what he was suggesting was impossible. He backed off.

"Well, at least be on your guard when you do. Just in case they come out looking for you. Mom's really curious now. You've got to make sure she never spots you."

✳   ✳

Jason could see that Mom was worried the moment she walked into the cabin that evening.

"Something wrong?" he asked.

She nodded. "We've just been told that Jan Slater from the *ORCA* Board is coming out here tomorrow. She wants to look at the results in certain laboratories, and we're on the list."

"So?"

"So, everyone knows what that means. They're cutting back on funding. Some of those labs are going to be closed down."

Brett looked over, frowning. "But if they shut your lab, what'd happen to us?"

Mom sighed. "Well, there'd be no reason for us to stay on *ORCA*. I guess we'd all have to go back to the mainland."

Seeing the alarm on both boys faces, Mom tried to sound reassuring. "I don't think we have to start packing our bags quite yet," she said. "As long as Winston and I can convince her that our work's making progress, I hope she'll see it's important we continue."

But Jason could hear the tremor of doubt in her voice, and a sudden fear gripped him. If Mom was wrong, it would mean saying good-bye to Neri, probably forever.

✳ ✳

The next day Neri was keeping Jason's cautionary words at their last meeting in mind. She and Charley were staying out of view of *ORCA* and traveling underwater, only coming up for air occasionally.

The boat bearing Jan Slater from the mainland was almost on top of them before Neri, surfacing first, saw it coming.

Dive. Dive deep, she called to him as she hurled

herself back down into the depths. But Charley was slow to respond. The very tip of the keel grazed along his back as the vessel passed over him. It clipped the tag behind his head with a harsh grating sound just as Charley made good his escape.

On board the boat, Jan Slater clutched the rail for support as the craft shuddered. Underwater, the transmitter light on Charley's tag fluttered and died.

Jason and Brett were keeping a wary eye on developments in Mom's lab when the sound of the whale song abruptly ceased. In the silence that followed, Winston called their attention to the screens.

"Look. We've lost the brain scan and the locater transmission as well. Everything's gone out!"

Dianne stared at the equipment in disbelief. "Oh no!" she groaned, "And Jan's going to be here in about twenty minutes! Come on, Winston, boost the receivers or something. We've got to get those signals back fast!"

They were still trying when Lucas ushered in Jan Slater through the door half an hour later.

"I hope you had a good trip out," Dianne smiled, edgily.

"There was a bit of excitement, actually," Jan replied. "We hit something in the water. Fortunately, it was just a bump so it didn't do any real damage."

She seemed pleasant enough to Jason as she was introduced to him and Brett, but when she turned back to Mom, it was all business.

"Well, Dianne, why don't you just show me what you've been up to?"

Mom tried hard, Jason had to grant her that. And Jan Slater seemed impressed by the whale song recording and the computer records of the accompanying brain patterns. But when Mom had to admit that their equipment had failed, Slater's face turned grim.

"I'll have to be honest with you," she said finally. "There are certain people on the Board who already regard your research as, well, a waste of money. If I go back and report to them that the millions of dollars worth of apparatus isn't even functioning, they won't hesitate. They'll close you down within a week."

Well, that's it, Jason thought to himself. We're finished.

But then Dianne piped up. "How long will you be here, Jan?"

"Until 1900 hours this evening."

There was a note of desperation in Dianne's voice. "If I can get everything working again before then, will you recommend we be allowed to continue?"

Jan nodded. "Yes, I think that would do the trick. I'd have to see it for myself, mind."

"You'll see it."

It wasn't until Lucas had escorted Slater out to her next appointment that Jason found voice to question his mother. How on earth did she mean to fix it all by then? Mom said she'd had an idea. Since all the lab equipment was still operational, as far as they could see, then the fault had to be with the tag on the whale. She turned to Winston with a question.

"You made up two of those tags, didn't you?"

"Yes," Winston said, "but only one was ever fitted with the dart assembly. We haven't got time to make another one now."

"We won't have to," Dianne replied coolly, "if we simply switch them over."

Jason stared at her. Had she gone completely crazy?

"Oh sure, Mom," Brett said, echoing his thoughts. "And how do you do that? Swim out and say, 'Hi Whale. Mind if I look at your tag and do a few repairs?'"

"More or less. I think we could use recordings of his own song to attract him. I'd wait underwater for him to come. Then if I could just get close enough, I could slip the old module out of the assembly and snap the new one in its place."

"You'd never get anywhere near it," Jason protested. "And you haven't dived in ages!"

But Mom was insistent. She couldn't let all their work go for nothing. She had to try. "Are you coming?" she asked Winston.

"Well, I'm certainly not letting you go alone."

"I'm coming, too," Jason said. "You need someone to drive the boat, Mom. And a diving partner."

She looked at him hard for a moment. "Very well," she said, "but the minute that whale appears, I want you out of the water. Winston, get the new module and a submarine transmitter. I'll choose the recordings. Brett, help Jason fetch the scuba gear. All meet up on the platform. Quickly!"

✳   ✳

Winston was carefully lowering an underwater speaker over the side of the boat as Jason and Dianne finished strapping on their air tanks.

"Watch your depths, won't you?" he was saying. "And don't try to race the whale. The human body does not respond to sudden ascents and descents like they do. Beware of 'Rapture of the Deep.'"

Dianne nodded impatiently and picked up the replacement module. "Wish us luck," she said to Brett, tousling his hair in passing. Then she and Jason plunged overboard and disappeared from sight.

"What's that rapture thing you were talking about?" Brett asked Winston as he followed the trail of bubbles marking their progress.

"'Rapture of the Deep.' It's something all divers risk. It makes them light-headed and foolish. Sometimes, they even forget they have to breathe.

But don't worry, my boy. I'm sure they will look after each other."

He picked up the first recording and loaded it into the transmitter. "Well, here goes."

Underwater, the sound of whale song burst from the speakers, its call reverberating through the canyons of the ocean.

❋ ❋

Neri stood on the beach at Charley's Cove, puzzled. He had disappeared without warning, and now she could hear not one but two songs in her head. Yet both sounded like Charley. It was most strange.

She walked into the water and began to make her way out to sea.

❋ ❋

Winston gave a whoop of delight and called Brett over to the Lanar screen. He tapped at the large fuzzy blip entering the area. "It's him, and he's heading straight for us!"

❋ ❋

Jason felt Mom nudge his arm. She indicated her watch and then the tanks on her back. Finally, she pointed to him and jerked a thumb upward. Jason got the message.

With a nod, he began to kick slowly and easily upward. As he rose, he watched the outline of the boat far above him, slowly getting larger as he ascended. He was unaware of another shape, a great dark form moving in from the east toward them.

Jason surfaced, threw his flippers aboard, and climbed the small ladder on the boat's side.

"We were beginning to run a bit low on air," he explained. "She told me to come up for new tanks."

Winston picked up a spare set of empty cylinders lying on the deck. Jason began to take off his own tanks for refilling as Winston moved to start the compressor.

"This will take a while," he warned.

"No problem," Jason said. "She's still got plenty left. And there's nothing happening down there."

In the sea below, Jason had only just disappeared from sight when Dianne saw the whale. It cruised into sight and then began slowly circling the boat underwater, curious but cautious.

Gripping the module, Dianne swam slowly forward toward it. She came up behind the gigantic body, careful to avoid the undulating flukes. Edging her way toward the head, she could actually make out the broken module, trailing from the tag. A dozen more strokes and she actually would be able to touch it.

Then, without warning, the whale rolled and dived. Dianne dived after it, anxious to keep up. The creature leveled out and seemed to pause again. Once more, Dianne started to approach the head when, with a flick of the giant tail, it moved away, this time upward.

She watched in disbelief. The darned thing was

playing with her! Determined, she set off after it again.

It was on their third ascent, a particularly fast one, that the strange sensations started to hit her. Her head went giddy. The murky darkness of the seafloor seemed to suddenly glow with bright, enchanting colors. The whale appeared to change size, shrinking down until it was no bigger than a goldfish. She felt the module slipping from her grasp and dropping away toward the ocean floor below, but this struck her as funny rather than alarming. She was consumed with an uncontrolled urge to laugh.

Rapture of the Deep.

As she tore the mask from her face, the whale's great black eye swiveled around to watch her.

Neri, he called, *come. A creature is in peril.*

Some distance away, Neri paused underwater as she heard the call. She concentrated. There was the figure in a strange suit like the one she had seen Jason wear. And as the breathing tube fell away from its mouth, she recognized the face. It was Mother.

Neri launched herself forward at high speed.

Winston was just finishing filling Jason's tanks when a shout from Brett drew their attention. Brett pointed to the steady stream of bubbles coming up from the sea below. One glance told Jason something was terribly wrong. He grabbed the replenished spare cylinders from the deck and frantically began to wrestle them onto his back.

Below, Dianne was beginning to drift helplessly downward when Neri reached her. Catching her in one arm, Neri clutched the floating air hose with her free hand and forced the mouthpiece back between her lips. Then she began to ascend at a slow, steady rate.

"She's coming up!"

Brett's call came just as Jason was about to leap overboard. He hurried to the stern of the boat to see for himself. Sure enough, a shadowy shape was coming up from below. But it seemed to him there was something strange about it.

A few moments later Neri broke the surface, still holding Dianne under one arm. Jason was aware of Winston beside him. He stood rooted to the spot, staring at Neri, his eyes popping and his mouth agape.

Dianne's body was limp and her head hung but, to his relief, Jason could hear the suck of air through her air tube. He reached down and caught hold of her. Winston managed to force his frozen limbs into motion and came to help the two boys. As they eased Mom over the side, Neri looked a fearful question to Jason. He nodded, both in thanks and in reassurance that she would be all right.

The next time Winston looked, the girl had disappeared.

Dianne lay on the deck coughing and spluttering

as they gathered anxiously around her. Her eyelids fluttered then came half open. She looked blearily up at Winston. Her voice, when she finally spoke, was a weak whisper.

"The girl," she croaked. "Did you see her?"

"Yes," Winston said quietly, "I saw her."

Dianne nodded and closed her eyes again, exhausted. As Winston hurried to raise the anchor for the return journey to *ORCA* and medical help, Jason and Brett looked at each other.

"Well," Jason said, under his breath, "The cat's out of the bag now."

❋   ❋

In the UBRI laboratories on the mainland, Hellegren lifted his head from the bank of instruments over which he was poring. The sound of whale songs rang clear in the air.

"You know, Johansson," he said to his assistant, "the more I hear of these recordings, the more I think there is something rather special about this particular whale."

"Doctor?"

"In all my experience, I have never encountered a specimen that communicated with such clarity and frequency. If ever a creature was going to help us unlock their language, this one is it. I would dearly like to examine it more closely."

Johannson laughed. "Perhaps we could invite it over for afternoon tea, sir."

Hellegren's face was stony. "I am not joking, my

friend. For the moment, Dr. Bates's research is enough for our immediate needs. But the day may soon come when it is no longer sufficient. To probe deeper, we will need the animal itself in our hands."

A cool glint lit his eye as he added, "And if we want the creature, we will have to be prepared to *take* it."

CHAPTER TWELVE

THE MEETING

As they wheeled Dianne through the *ORCA* corridors toward the infirmary, the boys followed the trolley. Although she still looked pale, she beckoned Jason closer. "You weren't lying, were you? She really is out there?"

Jason glanced at all the medical staff surrounding them and tried to sound as natural as possible. "Don't say anything, Mom. You've been through a bad time, that's all. Save your strength."

"Your son's right. Dr. Bates," the chief medical officer agreed. "For the next couple of hours you must do nothing but rest."

Jason and Brett watched as she was wheeled away into the infirmary.

* *

"Mother will be all right?" Neri asked anxiously, almost before the boys had stepped ashore.

"Yeah, they say she's gonna be fine," Jason replied, as he and Brett clambered out of the boat. "They're just gonna keep her in observation for a few hours to make sure. But it's only thanks to you, Neri."

Brett began to add his thanks, too, but Neri interrupted him. She had a volley of questions she wanted answered. Why did Charley have two voices at once? What was Mother doing underwater? Why was she chasing him with another "little arrow"?

As they sat on the beach, Jason and Brett explained all. When they came to the need to replace the broken module on Charley's tag, Neri appeared troubled.

"Is important?" she asked.

"Well, Mom's job was hanging on it," Jason confessed.

"Yeah," Brett wailed, "and now we've blown it, we'll be thrown off *ORCA*."

Neri looked to Jason in disbelief. "You go away? Won't come back?"

"We won't really have much choice, Neri," he answered glumly.

"Then I mend it. You show me how."

With the aid of a crude diagram drawn in the sand, Jason demonstrated how the old module was released from the tag and a new one clicked into its place. But, he added, it was too late for that now, since Mom had dropped the only one left and it was now lying somewhere out on that vast ocean floor. It could by anywhere, he pointed out hopelessly.

Neri was undaunted. "Charley and I can find it. You go back and care for Mother."

With that she strode into the sea, plunged in, and disappeared from their sight.

On the return journey, the boys agreed on their strategy. They would play dumb, admit nothing if possible. Perhaps, on recovering, Mom would think Neri was just a hallucination, part of the rapture that had overcome her. As for Winston, well, they would cross that bridge when they came to it. Maybe they could still bluff their way out of this.

Many miles away, Neri plucked the silver object from a rocky outcrop near the seabed and began to carry it up toward Charley, drifting near the surface above.

Dianne was already out of the infirmary when Jason and Brett arrived back at *ORCA*. They found her in her laboratory, arguing with Jan Slater. Commander Lucas looked on. In the background, Winston was still fiddling with their control panels, vainly trying to raise some sign of response.

As the boys entered, Mom shot them a look so intense that Jason was unnerved. But then she ignored them, turning back to Jan.

"You've heard how good our tapes are up to date," she pleaded. "This is the most important project I've ever worked on in my life, Jan. You can't let them close us down now."

Jan sympathized and said she would do her best to convince the Board. "But I can't hold out much hope," she added. "If only you hadn't had this major breakdown, things would be different."

Lucas tapped his watch and told Jan Slater that her boat back to the mainland would be waiting. Jan nodded. "I'm sorry, Dianne," she said in parting and turned for the door.

And just then, suddenly, all their equipment burst back into life. The sound of whale song erupted from the speakers. The recorders began to spin. On the locator screen, the large blip that was Charley could clearly be seen, with the smaller one moving alongside.

Slater stared, frowning. "How on earth did that happen?"

"There is a very wise old saying," Winston chimed in. "Do not question a miracle, for the truth may be even more unbelievable."

Dianne looked Jan square in the eye. "Well, looks like you'll have to change your report now, doesn't it?"

Jan smiled. "It seems you're going to be stuck with this lot for a while longer, Commander Lucas."

And for once, even Lucas managed a slight grin.

144

As Lucas ushered Jan from the lab, Jason and Brett began to follow, wishing to make themselves scarce. But Mom barred their way.

"Oh no, you don't," she said, closing the door. "Now it's time for us to have a long talk about your strange little girlfriend. Sit down."

Within minutes, Jason sensed they were doomed. Their attempts to look vague or stupid were met with hard looks of disbelief from Mom.

"I want the truth," she demanded with dangerous calm.

"Where on earth does she come from?" Winston asked, more gently.

Jason made one last-ditch effort. "She's just a cleaner," he lied. "We don't know anything else about her." But Mom's reaction was cool and skeptical.

"Oh really, Jason? I'll tell you what I know, then."

She began to count off on her fingers.

"I know she can swim to extraordinary depths at unbelievable speeds without any breathing apparatus. Correct?"

The boys sat silent. Mom tapped another finger.

"Since she managed to lift me to the surface alone without any effort, I'd have to presume she's unusually strong."

No reply. Mom touched the third finger, then paused for a moment, as if unsure of voicing it herself.

"And she is the little creature on that screen, isn't she? She can . . . communicate with the whale!"

She waited for an answer. When none came, she sighed and crouched so her head was level with theirs. "Boys," she said quietly, "if you don't give me the answers, I'll have to get them another way. One word about this to Lucas and he'll have half of *ORCA* out tracking her down. Believe me, it's the last thing I want to do, but you'll leave me no choice if you won't level with me."

Jason and Brett exchanged a glance. They were trapped. And so, with reluctance, they began to relate the whole sequence of events from the beginning. They told of Neri's island, though refused to reveal the location. They explained what they had learned of her strange and unclear past, and the childhood accident that led to her long friendship with Charley.

Mom and Winston listened in silence. Only when they had finished did Mom finally speak. "Tomorrow, first thing in the morning, I want you to go to this island and ask her if she'll come and meet me here."

Jason opened his mouth, but she cut him short. "Don't tell me you can't get her on board, Jason, because you've obviously done it before. I just want to talk to her, that's all."

"I'll see what she says. But first, you both have to swear that you won't tell anyone else about her."

Mom pointed out that she and Winston had

more reason than anybody to keep the secret. "This girl could help put our research miles in front of anyone else in the field. Do you really think we'd want our competition getting wind of what she can do?"

Brett still looked uneasy. "You wouldn't hurt her at all, would you?"

"Don't be silly. Of course not."

"Just go easy on her. Neri's kinda special."

Mom put her arm around his shoulders. "She's more than special, Brett." Her eyes met Winston's as she continued. "She's potentially the most amazing thing biological science has seen this century."

✳   ✳

Neri stood in the lab doorway, wearing the *ORCA* uniform that had once been Vanessa's. She was flanked on either side by Jason and Brett. Dianne walked over, a little unsurely, Jason thought, and held out her hand.

"Neri? I'm . . ."

"Mother." Neri finished the sentence for her. She took the proffered hand awkwardly and stared closely, as though comparing the paleness of it with the sun-bronzed skin of her own.

Dianne led her across and introduced her to Winston, then placed her in a chair and sat down opposite.

"First of all, I want to thank you for what you did for me yesterday." Neri just shrugged with a smile. "Secondly, I want to ask for your help. You're a phenomenon, Neri."

Neri looked to the boys. "What is phen-omen-on?"

"Something really different," Jason explained.

"Ultraradical," Brett added.

"You could be of very great assistance to us in our work," Dianne went on, "but first, we'd like to find out a lot more about you. They're just routine tests. We'd never try to make you do anything you don't want to. Trust me."

"Of course I trust," Neri replied simply. "You are Mother."

"Then you will help us?"

Neri nodded. And so Dianne set to work.

Jason and Brett insisted on staying to keep a watch on proceedings, but nothing happened that first day to cause them any alarm. Neri was measured, weighed, and had her eyesight and hearing examined. It was during the latter that she suddenly stiffened, and cocked her head to one side, curiously.

"Is something the matter, Neri?" Dianne asked, noticing the movement.

"Charley is calling me. Is worried."

The room was silent. All the equipment had been switched off so as not to interfere with the high frequency sounds with which Neri was being tested. Dianne nodded to Winston. He walked over and flicked the controls. A low, moaning call issued from the speakers. The large blip hovered near the very edge of the screen. Dianne looked back at Neri.

"You could hear him? Even at that distance?"

"Yes," said Neri, as though puzzled at the question. "I tell him to go home and wait for me."

She seemed lost in concentration for a few moments, humming under her breath so softly it could hardly be heard. In response, the blip began to move away, out of range.

Dianne stared at it, awestruck. "If I wasn't seeing this for myself, Winston," she said in a whisper, "I'd say it was impossible."

Winston gave a little smile. "I think this young lady is about to teach us that impossible is a word we scientists should avoid."

At 1730 hours that afternoon Jason called a halt. Neri had to be off *ORCA* before the other day-pass workers left, he explained. He and Brett escorted her up to the platform.

After she had changed and the uniform was safely stowed, they walked together to the edge. "I come again tomorrow," she said.

"You don't have to, you know, Neri," Jason pointed out, "I only said I'd ask you to come once."

"Oh, but I want to! Now I can be with you and Brett and Mother, have . . . family."

Her eyes glittered like rays of sunlight dancing on waves. "Tomorrow," she repeated, smiling, and dived into the ocean.

Jason stared after her, bemused, then turned to Brett. "Of all the families you could choose," he mused, "who the heck would want ours?"

✳   ✳

It was late in the evening and Brett was hurrying back to their cabin. He had been air-surfing with Froggy and Zoe. This was a totally illegal activity entailing crawling out on a grille over the main ventilator shaft and letting the powerful upward draft lift you off your feet. Once airborne, you could hover, spin, even do somersaults. Froggy was too chicken to attempt it himself, but acted as judge of the best performance. Zoe always won.

Anxious to be home in time in case Mom started asking questions, Brett took a shortcut through the biology department. The corridor was in semi-darkness and Brett was just passing the door of Mom's lab when he heard faint sounds coming from within. He stopped, paused, then put his ear to the door. Yes. There was the soft shuffle of feet and then a click as though some piece of machinery was being turned on. He knew it couldn't be Mom or Winston because they'd closed up for the day. Someone else was in the lab, and they had no right to be there. Brett moved away on tiptoe until he was out of earshot and then ran for home.

"If this is one of your jokes, Brett, you're going to be sorry," Jason hissed as Mom led them up to the lab floor, the key card in her hand. She unlocked the door and turned on the lights. The room was empty. No sign of life at all. "Honest, Mom!" Brett insisted, as they looked around.

She raised an eyebrow. "The door was locked, and nothing's missing. So how and why would anyone be in here?"

"I dunno," he insisted, "but they were."

She considered him wryly. "I think we'll put it down to an overactive imagination, Brett. But let's not have it happen again, hmm?"

Locking the door again, she led the way back to their cabin.

✳   ✳

Johannson switched off the latest whale song recording and put it back in its cover. "This one is dated only three weeks ago," he noted to Hellegren. "Very soon we'll have caught up to Dr. Bates's current work. Your contact on *ORCA* does a good job."

Hellegren did not answer. He was intent, pouring over a mapping screen, making calculations at the same time. Johannson strolled across and peered over Hellegren's shoulder. On the screen was a satellite image of the UBRI building and the cliffs leading to the bay below. But a further detail had been computer imposed, a straight line connecting both arms of the bay, sealing it off from the ocean beyond.

"What is this?" Johannson asked.

"An electronic fence," Hellegren replied calmly, "similar to the sort of thing some farmers still use to stop cattle from straying. Except this one can be raised or lowered as the need arises. Installation is to begin immediately."

"Is this to stop something from getting into the bay?"

"It's stopping things getting out I'm concerned with. Once the net is raised, nothing inside that fence is going to escape back to sea."

Johannson started to understand. "Not even a whale?" he asked.

Hellegren bared his teeth in a mirthless smile. "Oh, especially not a whale."

CHAPTER THIRTEEN
SEA CHANGE

In the days that followed, Neri became a constant visitor to *ORCA*. Every morning Jason and Brett would wait for her, make sure the coast was clear, then usher her aboard and down to the laboratory where Mom was waiting. Later they would collect her again and watch as she set off home to the island.

One afternoon, when they arrived to say it was time for Neri to leave, Dianne snapped. It was impossible to work with the constant comings and goings, she said. And since many of the whales in the area were already leaving on the great migration south, their time of having contact with Charley could be running out. She took Neri's hands and looked into her eyes.

"Neri, if I could arrange it, how would you like to stay here on *ORCA* for a little while?"

There was a note of excitement in Neri's voice. "Stay with family?"

"Yes."

"I like it very much."

Dianne got on the communicator to Commander Lucas. She had a young lady who was assisting them with their research, she explained, and it was vital that she be on call when needed. Therefore, they would like her to be issued with a resident's pass. Lucas frowned. It was most unusual, he said. Besides, he doubted there were any spare berths to allocate. "There's an extra bunk in my cabin," Dianne insisted. "I'll take full responsibility for her."

Lucas seemed to waver.

Dianne played her master stroke. "If necessary, I'll take the matter to Jan Slater and the Board."

Lucas gave an exasperated sigh. "Oh, all right, then. I'll clear it with personnel. Give them the details and have the ID card made up." The screen went black.

That night Neri lay awkwardly on the unfamiliar softness of a mattress while Mom moved to turn off the reading lamp. "We have a big day tomorrow," she said.

Neri smiled as she turned off the light. Lying in the dark, Neri thought she could hear Charley singing and sang back, *I am here. I will return soon.*

But in the excitement of the moment, his call seemed oddly distant, moving further away.

At breakfast next morning little attention was paid to Neri. Vanessa regarded her with the usual suspicion and Lee seemed a bit put out to see her arrive with Jason, but the others were too busy talking about the upcoming *ORCA* Junior Dance. The dance was a major social event and the air was thick with discussion of what clothes would be worn and who would be partnering whom. Neri sat and listened in fascination as she ladled spoonfuls of revegiton into her mouth.

At the next table, however, more sinister matters were under consideration. "Mom doesn't believe me," Brett was saying to Froggy and Zoe, "but I swear to you, I heard someone in her lab the other night."

"But if the door's locked, how are they getting in?" Zoe asked.

"Search me. But they are doing it somehow."

"There's one way to find out," Froggy said calmly. "A movement detector."

"Who's got one of those?"

"I have. I made it years ago for my grade four science project. Oh, and we'll need something else. Talcum powder."

That evening, Brett slipped Dianne's key card into his pocket and joined his friends outside the lab. Using the card, they entered. Starting from the far side of the room, they scattered a fine layer of powder across the floor, working their way back toward the door. When they had finished Froggy put a metal cube with an electronic eye on a bench nearby and produced a remote monitor. When he waved his hand in front of the device, a light on the monitor began to flash. Satisfied, Froggy reset it. Then they shut the door and retreated into a shadowy alcove down the corridor.

They had lost track of how long they had been there when suddenly Zoe grabbed Froggy's arm and hissed urgently, "Froggy! Look!" She pointed. The light on the monitor was flashing. They ran for the door. As Brett fumbled with the card, they could hear scurrying sounds inside, followed by a metallic clang. Brett got the door unlocked and they hurried in.

At first glance the place looked deserted, but a stack of Dianne's whale song recordings taken from their shelves and hastily abandoned, showed that someone had been there. On the bench beside them lay an appliance that Froggy recognized immediately as a high-speed dubbing machine for making copies. And then they saw footprints in the powder. They led from the air-conditioning duct in the wall and out again the same way. The grille was hanging loosely in its mounts. They tore if off and scrambled inside in pursuit.

The chute they found themselves crawling along was narrow and dark, but they could hear bumping and clanging, as someone ahead of them clumsily hurried to escape. When they came to a point where the shaft divided into two, they split up, Froggy and Zoe going one way, Brett the other. Froggy and Zoe were going full pelt when suddenly the shaft dropped down underneath them at a steep angle. It was too late to stop. "Ahhh!" they yelled in unison, as they slid helplessly downward, picking up speed as they went.

They hit the grille at the bottom with such force that they knocked it out and spilled on to the floor on the far side. They sat up, shaking their heads. To their horror, they realized they were sitting on the floor of Lucas's cabin while he, in his underwear and a pair of old slippers, sat staring at them, thunderstruck.

In the meantime, Brett saw light coming from the end of the shaft that he had followed. The grille had been removed. Obviously, this was where the intruder had got out. Brett followed suit and found himself in a corridor. He hurried along it and emerged in the reception area.

The movement of the main elevator door closing caught his eye. He looked across—just in time to catch a glimpse of the handsome but frightened face of Billy Neilson before the door shut and he was whisked away.

By the time the elevator returned and Brett got up to the platform, all he could see was the receding lights of a small boat as it disappeared into the inky night.

A computerized image of Billy's face looked down at them from the communicator screen in the lab.

"Wilhelm Neilson," Lucas said. "According to our records, he came on board just over six weeks ago to work in the computer division. It was obviously a front, though. He was clearly planted here by someone."

"Can't you find him?" Brett asked.

"We've located the boat he took. It was left at a jetty on the mainland. But he appears to have gone to ground." He looked across to where Dianne and Winston were checking their equipment.

"Anything else missing, Dr. Bates?"

"It doesn't seem so."

"Then he came specifically to copy those recordings of yours. And that's what really puzzles me. With all due respect, Doctor, who would go to such lengths to get them? And why?"

"I don't know," Dianne replied. "I wish I did."

✳   ✳

Jason had been left in their quarters to look after Neri. "Jason," she asked, out of the blue. "What is this dance?"

"You must know what dancing is, Neri?"

"No. You tell me."

"Well, a lot of kids get together and jump up and down and wave their arms about and stuff like that."

Neri scowled. "Why?"

"Look, it might be easier if I show you." Jason got his octophonic player from his cabin. He selected a microdisc and dropped it into the slot. "Come on, you stand opposite and follow me."

At first Neri looked so stiff and uncomfortable that Jason found it hard not to laugh. But he urged her on. "Just move your feet in time to the music. Now let the rest of your body go with it." By the time Mom entered, Neri was starting to get the hang of it and grinning all over her face.

"Sorry to interrupt you two, but we've sorted out that business with Lucas, so it's time to get back to work now, Neri."

Jason objected. "Oh, give her a break, will you? She can't work all the time."

"Jason, we've lost hours this morning as it is. We're on the verge of some very important new research and we need her help."

"Well, maybe she doesn't want to. Maybe she'd rather come out to the island with me."

Neri broke in. "No, I go to the island tomorrow, perhaps. Today I help Mother as she asks."

"There, you see? I really don't know what's got into you, Jason."

"She's not just something for you to research! You're treating her like one of your specimens!"

"I object to that. Ever since the day I found her . . ."

"You didn't find her, Mom," Jason pointed out, levely, "and neither did I. 'Cause she was never

159

lost until she met us." He walked unhappily from the room.

❋   ❋

Billy Neilson stood apologetically in front of Dr. Hellegren at UBRI headquarters. He was sorry, he said, that his presence had been detected before he had got all of the whale song tapes. Hellegren waved his apologies aside. "You earned your money, my boy. We have sufficient for our present needs."

They both looked up as Johansson entered. "Well?" Hellegren asked keenly, "How are things progressing down at the bay?"

"The fence is nearly in place. The supervisor says a week at the most."

"Good."

"You really think this will work?"

"Johansson, according to Billy here, it was common knowledge that Dr. Bates used her recordings to get the whale to come to her. Well, we now have the very same recordings"—he patted the pile of covers stacked on the bench in front of him—"so it is simply a matter of following suit. Attract the creature's attention, draw him into the bay, and he is ours."

❋   ❋

Several nights later, Jason and Brett lay awake in their cabin, talking softly.

"Have you noticed that Neri's kind of changing?" Jason said. "She always seemed to be getting

160

messages from Charley but she's hardly mentioned him for days now. And she hasn't been back to the island ever since she came to stay on board. It's like she's, I dunno, switching off, somehow."

"Yeah," Brett sighed. "I'm beginning to wish things'd stayed the way they were, before any adults interfered."

✳   ✳

Neri half woke and sat up. For a moment, she thought she was being called by someone. But it must have been a dream. She looked over at the sleeping form on the other bunk. Mother. And in the other cabin, Jason and Brett. She was with her family. She was home.

With a little smile to herself, she rolled over and went back to sleep.

CHAPTER FOURTEEN
THE DANCE

Daggy was carrying a box of streamers as he passed Neri and the boys in a corridor. "Hey, we're starting to set up the recreation room for the rage tonight. You guys want to come and help?"

"Sorry, Dags, can't." Jason replied. "We've got something else to do."

"Oh." He turned his attention to Neri. "Well, I'll see you there, Neri. Might even get in a dance or two, eh?"

With a show of coolness, he stepped casually back and fell over a bulkhead. He picked himself up and, red-faced, continued on his way.

Jason happily led the way toward the main elevator. At last Neri had agreed to come with them to the island for the day. The boat was waiting above, fueled and ready to go. It would be like old times again.

And then Mom appeared. She wanted Neri to stay to do a few more tests, she said. To Jason's frustration, Neri agreed.

"You don't have to do everything she asks, you know," he said, when Dianne was out of earshot.

Neri looked puzzled. "But she is Mother."

"Ours, not yours," Jason pointed out, but when he saw the stung look on her face, he was sorry he'd opened his mouth. "Well, we'll still go out there, anyway," he muttered to Brett.

"Maybe I come tomorrow," Neri said.

"You've been saying that for ages," Jason replied, disgruntled. He and Brett walked on, reluctantly leaving her behind.

✳   ✳

"Fish . . . bird . . . star . . . tree . . ."

Neri sat in a chair in the lab. On her head was a cap that formed a blindfold, with electrodes attached. Dianne sat in front of her, holding up cards with simple pictographs on them. Although she could not see, Neri was right on every occasion. Dianne came over to Winston, who was watching the brain scan.

"How does she do it?" she asked quietly.

Winston shrugged. "I'm not sure, but it appears she's bouncing some sort of signal through the mask and then receiving it back again. Almost like the echolocation her friend Charley uses."

"Have we got the results of her blood tests yet?"

"It will be another day or so. I thought it was wiser to send them to the mainland for analysis. If we had them done here, someone might start asking questions."

"You have more drawings?" Neri called.

"No, Neri," Dianne said, returning to her. "I think that's enough for the day. Let's go home and start getting you ready for the dance."

"I can go?" She sounded surprised.

"Of course. I've been thinking about what Jason said and perhaps he's right. It's time for you to have some fun for a change."

Neri still looked a little doubtful. She knew everyone else would be wearing special clothes.

"You leave that to me," Dianne smiled. "We'll knock them dead tonight."

"Well, I'm glad to hear you're so enthusiastic about this shindig, Dr. Bates," Lucas said as he entered, "because I need a couple of chaperones and you and Dr. Seth just volunteered."

Dianne pulled a face, but Lucas's attention was already distracted by the sight of Neri in the strange cap with its trailing wires.

"Who's this?"

"Neri. The girl I mentioned to you."

"What on earth are you doing to her?" he asked.

"It's highly technical, Commander, it would take too long to explain," she said. "Anyway, we're finished now."

164

As he left, Lucas paused in the doorway and looked back at the figure strapped into the odd apparatus. What he saw troubled him.

✳   ✳

Back in their cabin, Dianne took several dresses from hangers and held them up against Neri. "I brought these along because I imagined there might be occasions I could wear them," she said wryly. "I must have been crazy. It's a good thing for you that my grandmother taught me to sew." She selected a dress, picked up a large pair of scissors, and began to cut.

✳   ✳

Jason and Brett sat on the beach, watching Charley as he moved constantly back and forth between the arms of the cove. There was a long silence before Jason finally spoke.

"Let's face it, the island's just not the same without her here. It's all, I dunno, different, somehow. The fun's gone." He looked out toward where the whale continued its agitated circling. "I reckon he's missing her, too," he added.

Some distance away, out in the ocean, Hellegren finished lowering a high-powered hydro transmitter into the water behind the UBRI boat. He looked over to where his team of audio experts were gathered around the sound deck, with the recordings already loaded.

"Very well, turn it on."

Charley's song, intermingled with Neri's,

began to ring out through the depths.

On the island, Brett frowned as he saw the whale suddenly breach, then turn out to sea. He nudged Jason. "Hey, look. Where's he going?"

They both watched, puzzled as he dived and disappeared.

"He's heading our way!" Hellegren called excitedly, poring over a screen. He turned to the helmsman. "Wait until I give the word and then start to cruise landward, nice and slow. With a bit of luck, he'll follow us all the way in."

✳   ✳

Dianne circled Neri, examining the dress critically. "Well, the hem's not perfect, but at least it fits, more or less. Now to tackle the rest of you."

As she fussed with hairbrushes and makeup, Neri laughed at the transformation she could see taking place in the mirror.

Dianne smiled. "You know, just between us, I always wanted a daughter," she confessed. "Not that I don't love the boys, of course," she added hastily.

"More than work?" Neri asked, her face suddenly serious.

"Well, of course. What a question. Why do you ask?"

"Because I think sometimes they do not know that."

Dianne was rattled. At times the girl's bluntness was breathtaking. And yet she couldn't deny the seed of truth. Perhaps at times it did appear to the

166

boys that she put her career before them. . . .

A knock on the cabin door interrupted her thoughts. "Hey, we're back," Jason called. "Is Neri there?"

"Yes, but we're going to be a while longer. You two get dressed and go on ahead. We'll meet you at the dance."

Jason and Brett exchanged a shrug and went to change.

✳   ✳

"Slowly, slowly," Hellegren warned the helmsman. They were approaching land, and though the whale was still trailing them, they did not want it to take fright and run back to deeper water.

He punched in the UBRI headquarters code on the communicator. Johannson answered.

"We are approximately ninety minutes out from base and closing," Hellegren informed him. "Lower the fence and have all personnel standing by in position. No mistakes. This may be the only chance we get."

✳   ✳

ORCA's recreation room throbbed to the beat of music. On the dance floor, Brett, Froggy, and Zoe bobbed in unison while Jodie came past with an ever-changing series of partners. Even Vanessa, who'd spent most of the evening so far sitting alone, had finally been asked to dance. She now stood in one spot, shuffling self-consciously, while Winston pranced opposite her like a demented grasshopper.

Jason and Lee were chatting with Daggy at the refreshment table when Neri entered with Dianne. Jason turned, saw her, and gaped.

She stood in the doorway, looking around her uncertainly. The dress was familiar–Jason vaguely remembered Mom wearing one very like it–but everything else was different. Her hair, normally an unruly mass of tangled curls, was drawn back and piled upon her head. The ruddy glow of her bronzed skin had been softened, somehow, showing up the green of her eyes and the arch of her high cheekbones. On her feet were a pair of Mom's heeled shoes, in which she teetered slightly.

Jason crossed the floor and walked up to her. "Neri," he said in wonderment. "You look like a real girl!"

She smiled. He nodded toward the floor. "Want to dance?"

She let herself be led away as someone turned the music up.

✱　　　✱

The biology department was silent and there was a faint click as the master key card unlocked the door of the Bates laboratory.

Lucas let it close behind him and turned the lights on. There was something strange going on up here; he felt it in his bones. People breaking in to steal material. That odd experiment with the girl. There was more happening than met the eye, and it was his duty to find out what it was.

He seated himself at the computer terminal and, overriding the code, unlocked their research files. He scanned the list. None of the labels made sense to him. Except one. The girl's name, wasn't it?

He tapped in N-E-R-I and entered it.

✳   ✳

"He's in!" Hellegren called. "Raise the fence! Now!"

There was a simultaneous hum from both sides as huge drums began to turn, winding in the cables that supported the fence on either side. As they tautened, they began to lift the fence up out of the water until it formed a solid barrier across the mouth of the bay, blocking it off from the sea beyond. When it clicked into place, it stood ten feet above the waterline and extended below the surface almost to the seafloor.

"Now turn the power on," Hellegren ordered. In the main laboratory of the UBRI headquarters on the cliffs above, Johannson threw a lever. There was a faint crackle as power surged through the cables and into the mesh of the fence.

On the deck of the boat Hellegren flicked off the whale song and instructed his helmsman to head the vessel into dock. He looked back with satisfaction at the great dark shape beginning to circle in the water behind them.

The sudden silence confused Charley. He had followed Neri's call all the way to this strange place and now she was not singing anymore. He began to search for a way out. It was only then that he realized he was trapped.

✳   ✳

On *ORCA* the music had slowed to a gentler tempo, and Jason guided Neri carefully around the floor. She moved unsurely, but she was laughing and her eyes shone with pleasure.

And then she thought she heard a faint call from very far away, a barely audible cry of distress.

Jason frowned at the change that came over her face. "Are you all right?" he asked. She didn't answer. Puzzled, he took her hand again and continued dancing.

✳   ✳

A bank of flood lights lit up the bay. Hellegren looked down with satisfaction from the UBRI laboratory above. Johannson and Billy were with him. The whale was beginning to thrash the water with its mighty tail.

"I think he's going to make a run for it," Johannson observed.

"Let him try," replied Hellegren. "He'll soon change his mind when he touches that fence."

Charley could see the open sea beyond. He summoned all his strength to give one great cry of anguish.

Neri!

Then he launched himself toward the barrier.

✳   ✳

As the call burst into Neri's brain, she saw the

fence beginning to loom up in front of her eyes. She reeled back with a gasp, tearing free of Jason.

"Neri, what's the matter?"

"Charley," she said, in a voice numbed with fear. "I must go to him."

She could still see the fence as it came closer and closer. And then, Charley touched it.

Neri was flung backward by the burning, searing shock, scattering dancing couples as she went. She grabbed at a metal wall to steady herself. As she touched it, sparks shot from her fingers and showered to the floor. Jodie screamed. Froggy dived for cover. In the ensuing mayhem, Neri ran for the door. It took Jason and Brett several moments to recover and run after her. By the time they reached the main elevator the doors had closed and she was on her way out of *ORCA*.

Neri ran to the edge of the platform, kicked off her shoes, plunged into the water, and headed for the island.

Charley was gone. She stood on the beach at the cove, calling his name, listening desperately for an answer. But none came. Finally, she sank to her knees on the sand and fell silent, staring out to sea with hollow eyes.

She was still there when the boys arrived at first light the next morning. As they clambered out of the boat, they saw her, a forlorn and bedraggled figure still in the remnants of Mom's dress. They came and sat on each side of her.

"I stayed too long in your world," she said finally, without looking at them. "I stop hearing Charley. And now I have lost him forever."

"No, Neri," Jason said quietly. "We're going to find him again. And when we do, I swear we'll help you bring him back home."

CHAPTER FIFTEEN

RALLYING THE TROOPS

From what Neri had seen the night before, it seemed certain that Charley was penned up somewhere. The question was where. Brett was sure the theft of the whale song recordings had something to do with it. Jason tended to agree, and since that trail seemed to lead toward the mainland, he felt the search should concentrate in that direction. He suggested they follow the coastline while Neri attempted to call to him.

"But I can hear him no more, Jason," she said.

"Well, perhaps he's not singing as loud as usual," Jason shrugged. "Getting through to you like he did last night must've used up a lot of energy."

"Yeah, and it's got to take it out of him, being locked up like that," Brett added.

"If you get close enough, maybe you'll make contact again. Who knows? At least it's worth a try, isn't it?"

Neri thought about it for a moment, then stood. "I try. But I go alone. Will be faster."

Jason nodded. "All right, but before you go, I brought something for you."

He went to the boat and came back carrying a bundle. "Here." He handed it over. It was Neri's rough cloth shift. After she changed, she passed back the sodden remains of Dianne's dress. "Tell Mother I do not need anymore," she said. "Ever."

Jason could not help thinking how like the old Neri she looked as she strode into the water and disappeared beneath the waves.

❈   ❈

Dianne and Winston walked into the lab that morning and stopped in their tracks. Lucas was sitting at their computer terminal, staring at the screen. There were shadows under his eyes and he looked like a man who had not had a lot of sleep.

"Good morning. Dr. Bates," he said quietly, without looking up. "I've been waiting for you."

Walking across, she looked over his shoulder. On the screen was their main Neri file. It contained a detailed diary as well as records of her conversations with Charley and the results of their physical examinations. He had read it all.

"You realize that I must report this to my superiors immediately," he said.

"Commander, you can't do that."

"It's my duty, Dr. Bates. If even half of this is true, the girl has to be brought to their attention."

"The minute she becomes public knowledge, half the scientists in the world are going to be trying to get their hands on her."

"And you want to keep her for yourself, is that it?"

She felt her anger rising. "No!"

Lucas held her with a steady, questioning gaze.

"All right," she conceded reluctantly. "Perhaps that was a consideration in the beginning. But I've also gotten close to Neri. She's become like a daughter. And I don't want her turned into a freak show."

"It's a bit late for that, isn't it?"

"I need time to think this out. Please, Commander, just give me twenty-four hours."

Lucas got to his feet and headed toward the door.

"Twenty-four hours, Doctor," he said.

＊　　　＊

Neri had almost given up hope again when she heard the call. She was out to sea, following the coast, when the faint sound reached her ears. It sounded weak and weary but it was still Charley's song. A moment later, she had gauged the direction and was zooming through the water toward him.

She found him in the bay, lolling listlessly in his

prison behind the fence. She checked the barrier hopefully, but it was too high to jump, too deep to get under.

Keeping low in the water, she sang back to him. *Charley, I am here*.

He responded, his huge bulk coming around as he turned and nosed toward her. He came right up to the fence. She reached out to touch him and, as her hand brushed against the metal mesh, a pain like fire shot through her arm and jolted her whole body.

✳   ✳

Back on the island, Jason winced as he examined the burn mark on her palm. "There must be some kind of high-voltage current running through the thing," he said to Brett. "No wonder it's knocked Charley about."

Neri was preoccupied, drawing a crude sketch of the bay in the sand with a stick. "The burning thing goes here," she said, adding a line across the entrance. "Then big snakes go up to house on top."

Jason studied it. "They must be power cables. And they're coming from this place on the hill. If we could get in there and turn it off, we might be able to destroy the fence."

"Get real, will you?" Brett shook his head. "The three of us could never do that by ourselves. We'd need a whole gang."

"Right," Jason agreed, his jaw set grimly. "And that's just what we're going to get."

✳   ✳

"But shouldn't we at least tell Mom?" Brett hissed as they stepped out of the main elevator into the reception area.

Jason was adamantly against it. It was when adults had been allowed to interfere that everything had started going wrong, he reminded Brett. They were none of them to be trusted anymore. "That's why we stick to kids for this."

They split up. Jason sought out Daggy and Lee in the galley. "Hey, have you seen Neri anywhere around?" Daggy asked. "Everyone's talking about what happened last night."

Jason leaned toward both of them and lowered this voice. "You want to hear about Neri, be in the recreation room at 2200 hours tonight."

At the same time, Brett was talking to Froggy and Zoe. "All I can tell you is that it's something really big. So don't mention it to anybody else. And be there."

"Well, that's seven altogether, counting Neri," Jason said then they met him back in reception. "Anyone else?" They looked around. Jodie was coming toward them, buffing her nails as she went.

"What do you reckon?" Jason asked, nudging Brett.

"Her? Jace, she's a real airhead."

"Maybe, but we could do with the extra pair of hands, couldn't we?"

Jodie looked more than a little bewildered by the invitation, but agreed to attend. They swore her to secrecy, unaware that Vanessa had walked into reception at that moment, and was watching them with interest from a distance. After the boys had departed, Jodie felt a tap on her shoulder.

"That was quite a talk you were having with the Bates brothers," Vanessa said. "Care to let me in on what it was about?"

✳   ✳

The boys arrived at the lab with the intention of assuring Dianne that Neri was all right and there was nothing to worry about. Instead they heard the news about Lucas's discovery of the files.

"All the more reason to keep quiet about tonight," Jason commented as they walked away. "It's better for Mom now if she knows nothing."

✳   ✳

At 2200 hours the group of kids gathered expectantly in the normally deserted recreation room. When the last one had arrived, Jason instructed Brett to stand guard by the door and then began to address them.

"Well, some of you already know that we've got you here because of Neri. She needs all our help. But first, I have to tell you a few things about her." He paused for a second to draw breath, then went on. "I warn you, you're going to find this hard to believe. But Brett and I both swear every word of it's true. . . ."

In the UBRI laboratory, high above the bay, Hellegren sat studying the day's results.

"This is rather disturbing, gentlemen," he said to Johansson and Billy. "We are getting some remarkably clear language patterns from the creature, but at the same time it is weakening much faster than we ever imagined. If it keeps declining at this rate, we may have to resort to artificial stimulation."

"What's that mean, Doctor?" Billy asked.

"A deep probe placed right in the brain itself. We can force the specimen to keep communicating, even against its will."

"Wouldn't that kill the animal eventually?"

Hellegren shrugged. "But we would continue to gather information right up until the end. Perhaps even the vital breakthrough we're looking for. And you must understand, young man, there will always be sacrifices. That is the nature of science."

He turned back to his work.

✳   ✳

". . . So now, we have to help Neri get Charley out of this place. And, well, that's about the whole story."

Jason finished and waited nervously for a response. For a long time, there was none. The rest of the kids just sat there with glazed eyes and dropped jaws.

Finally Daggy found his voice. "She actually swims like a fish. You're not kidding, are you,

Jason." It was a statement rather than a question.

"No, Dags," Jason replied quietly, "I'm not kidding."

"And she really can talk to this whale?" Lee asked.

"Ask Brett."

"Everything he's told you is the dead set truth," Brett confirmed. "Come along tomorrow and you'll see for yourself."

"I knew it!" cried a triumphant voice suddenly. They all swung around to see Vanessa emerging from behind some lockers in the corner. "I knew there was something weird about that girl the moment she came on board!"

Jason gasped. "What are you doing here?"

"Who opened their big mouth?" Brett said, surveying the room accusingly. All eyes began to turn toward Jodie, who looked shame-faced.

"She just said she wanted to know what was happening. She didn't say she was going to spy!"

Brett snorted. "What else would you expect from her?"

To his surprise, Jason noticed a flicker of hurt in Vanessa's eyes, though she tried to cover it.

"Well, maybe I wouldn't *have* to if you lot ever included me in anything. But no. Even though it was my uniform you stole, you weren't going to let me in on it. I've always been the outsider, haven't I?"

"That's because you're such a creep," Brett pointed out.

"Oh, yeah?" she retaliated. "Well, if you think I'm a creep now, I wonder what you'll call me when I tell Lucas what you're up to. Come on, Jodie."

But Jodie stood firm. "No," she said. "I'm sick of you pushing me around. I'm staying here. If you rat on them, you've got to rat on me, too. And then you're not going to have a friend left in the world."

"Not that you had one in the first place," Brett commented.

In the uproar that followed, Jason and Lee did their best to calm things down. Finally, Jason took Vanessa aside and spoke to her quietly.

"Look, I'm not asking this for myself, I'm asking it for Neri. She needs help and she's never done you any harm. Just keep your mouth shut until we've got a head start tomorrow morning. We probably haven't got a hope in hell but at least let us try."

Vanessa looked at him imperiously and shook her head. "There's only one way you're going to get off *ORCA* without me telling."

"What's that?"

"I go with you. For once, I'm not going to be the one who misses out."

Jason looked unsure. "I dunno."

"Get it clear, Bates. Either I go, too, or nobody goes."

"What about the rest of you? Who's in?" Brett demanded, ignoring her.

Everyone put their hands up except Froggy.

"Jeez," he frowned, "it sounds kinda dangerous to me."

"Oh, stop being such a wuss, Froggy," Zoe said, then added to Jason, "He'll come."

Jason looked at the rest of the troop then back at Vanessa. Her eyebrow arched in question. Jason sighed.

"Well, it looks like eight of us."

❋ ❋

At 0400 hours, while the rest of *ORCA* slept, the eight met in a darkened store room as arranged. They loaded up with pocket communicators, laser metal cutters, and lengths of microfiber rope. Then they filed silently through the corridors and into the main elevator.

❋ ❋

Dawn was just beginning to streak the sky as their boat bobbed in midocean, waiting. There was a sudden explosion of water and Neri broke the surface on the port side. The others goggled as Jason and Brett waved in greeting. "I told you we'd bring some friends to help out," Jason called, indicating the group.

"Thank you, friends," Neri said solemnly. Jason revved the engines. With Neri going ahead, guiding the way, they turned toward the mainland.

The sun was starting to climb in the sky as they moored the vessel in a secluded inlet a little distance from the bay. From where they were, they could see the UBRI building on the clifftops above. Neri left them there and cruised underwater to the seaweed side of the fence where she stopped, crooning to Charley.

Be patient. Our friends have come to set you free.

The group moved stealthily to a point overlooking the bay. Below them, they could see Charley and the barrier that held him prisoner.

Jason surveyed the scene and held a hurried conference. "We'll need two groups with laser cutters at each end of the fence. Brett, you and Vanessa take this side. . . ."

Brett went to protest, but Jason cut him off. "We haven't got time to argue, just do it, will you? Daggy, you and Jodie work your way around to the far end. When you get the word, cut through those cables as fast as you can. Good luck and keep your fingers crossed."

The two parties set out. Jason looked at the remaining group. Himself, Lee, Froggy, and Zoe. Not exactly the Dirty Dozen, but they would have to make do.

"Well, here we go," he said.

They began the long, slow climb toward the UBRI building above.

CHAPTER SIXTEEN
UBRI

Inside the laboratory, Hellegren examined the results of monitoring on the whale overnight and shook his head.

"We can't allow this to go on much longer," he said. "The creature is hardly communicating at all now, and his vital functions are beginning to fail. At this rate, we'll lose him by the end of the day. I think we had better prepare to insert the probe within the next hour."

"What will you need?" Johannson asked.

"The boat plus two Zodiac dinghies with divers and crew. Oh, and the helicopter to help herd him toward us."

"I'll order them to start standing by."

As Johannson went to the communicator

screen, Hellegren began to prepare the probe. It was a cylindrical device mounted on a long thin needle studded with electrodes. It ended in a sharp, cruel point. Billy came over, looking at it, disturbed.

"Dr. Hellegren, isn't there some other way? When we started out, you never said anything about this being done."

"Young man, I agree it is unfortunate. But this animal is leading us toward the very key of his species' language. The final clues may lie deep in his brain. And whatever the cost, we must try to get that information."

✳   ✳

Jason and his group peered at the UBRI building from behind a boulder, catching their breath. It had been an arduous climb, and more than once Jason had been tempted to heed Froggy's pleas and use the dirt road that ran from the top of the cliff to the bottom. But the risk of being spotted was too great, he had decided, and they had kept to the shelter of the rocks.

The building was surrounded on all sides by a high wire fence. A thickset uniformed guard stood at the gateway. There was no way they were going to get past him without being challenged.

Froggy pulled a Superscope from the knapsack full of tools he carried on his back. He focused in on the front door of the building. "Uh-oh," he muttered, "AZ 3000 computerized locking system.

185

Even if we could get to it, overriding the program could be tricky."

Jason looked back down at the bay below them. He could see the barrier jutting out of the water and knew that Neri was in position somewhere on the other side, waiting. But things weren't looking promising.

Zoe slid over beside him. "Why don't we just rush that bozo in the uniform?" she suggested. "There's four of us and only one of him."

Jason rolled his eyes. "Crazy idea, Zoe. The guy's the size of a minibus. Anyway, he'd see us coming a mile off."

"Jason," Lee nudged him. A number of men were coming out of the building. Some were in uniform, others in lab coats. Many carried equipment of one kind or another. They paused and spoke to the guard, who joined the group as it started to move off toward the path. "Get set, Froggy, here's our chance."

Froggy looked anxious. "Is it too late to change my mind about this?" he asked.

"Yes," Jason replied.

The group rounded the corner of the building and disappeared. "All right, now!" They ran forward, crouched low, passed through the gate, and made it safely to the front door.

While the others kept watch, Froggy pored over the electronic lock and then began to fiddle with it.

On one arm of the bay below, Daggy and Jodie

began to make their way into a mangrove swamp. Daggy was armed with a laser cutter and pocket communicator. Jodie with a hairbrush, nail file, and lipstick, which she was using up with the aid of a hand mirror.

"Why are you bothering?" Daggy asked.

"You never know who we could meet," she replied.

"In a swamp?" Daggy shook his head incredulously as they trudged on.

The bush on the other side was dense and scrubby. "You've got us lost," Brett said accusingly. "Why did I have to be stuck with you?"

"We're not lost, we just don't know where we are," Vanessa retorted. "And don't think I like your company, either, you little jerk."

"Don't call me a jerk, you dipstick!" The insults continued to fly as they floundered through the undergrowth.

"Come on, Froggy, come on," Jason pleaded.

"This isn't easy," Froggy pointed out. He had removed a plate from the side of the lock and was busy tampering with the circuitry within. "You'll just have to be patient." The others continued to keep watch, holding their breath.

✳   ✳

"The boys have disappeared," Dianne said to Winston as he arrived at the lab. "Some other kids, too, it seems. They're just working out exactly who." She was trying to keep her voice calm, but Winston was aware of the tension in it.

"But where would they have gone?"

"I'm sure it's something to do with Neri," she replied, then added bitterly, "so, of course, they wouldn't confide in *me*." Suddenly her emotions spilled over. "Am I that big a risk? Do they actually believe she's just a specimen to me, that I don't really care about her?"

Winston came over and sat beside her. "I think that is the very question you have to ask yourself right now," he said quietly.

"What do you mean?"

"I have given the matter some thought. We cannot prevent Commander Lucas from informing his superiors about Neri. But all the evidence of her powers—even the proof that she actually exists—is in those files over there."

He nodded toward the computer. It took Dianne a few moments to realize what Winston was getting at. When she did, she stared at him in disbelief.

"Are you suggesting we destroy our own research? As a scientist, I couldn't do that."

"As a scientist, no. It would mean concealing the greatest discovery of your career. But as the person that girl trusts and thinks of as a mother, you must. To protect her from the rest of the world."

She put her head in her hands. "Oh, Winston, what am I supposed to do?"

"I am afraid," he replied softly, "that is something only you can decide."

Froggy punched the air in jubilation as the door slid open with a soft hiss. Jason led the way as they slipped furtively inside.

They found themselves passing a series of empty laboratories. Clearly, the people who worked in them had been part of the group they saw departing earlier. But they could hear the muffled sound of voices coming from behind one door at the end of the corridor.

Jason cautiously edged up to it, the rest flattening themselves against the wall behind him. He reached for the door handle and slid it open an inch. Then he put his eye to the crack.

A tall man with silver hair was talking to half a dozen others. He was referring to a thin, spiked metal object on the bench in front of him.

"Remember, it must be driven all the way home in one thrust. And artificial stimulus must begin immediately."

Jason looked around the room. It was a large laboratory, much bigger and better equipped than any of the others they had passed. He felt a shock of recognition as he saw Billy Neilson, standing a bit apart from the others, but that was quickly forgotten when his eye fell on what lay beyond. In one corner of the room, a huge power plant hummed. Cables leading from it trailed across the floor and out a side door toward the cliff. They had found the power source for the fence.

At that moment, there was the clatter of a helicopter passing overhead. Hellegren glanced at his watch.

"Well, gentlemen," he said, "it appears the time has come. Only Johannson need stay here to keep an eye on the monitors. All the rest of the staff are already in position down below. Shall we join them?"

Carrying the metal object, the men began to come toward the door. Jason pulled his head back and quickly indicated to the others to get out of sight. They scattered down the corridor, looking for somewhere to hide. Zoe slid a door open. It was a cleaner's cupboard. They piled in and got the door shut just as they heard the party emerging from the laboratory. Sitting in the dark, the kids listened to them pass and head out through the main door. Then they began to make plans.

✳   ✳

On *ORCA*, Dianne sat in front of the computer screen, looking at the files she had called up. There they were, all the records they had ever made that contained any information about Neri. One jab of a finger and they would be no more.

She looked across to Wintson. "This is your work, too. Are you sure you want to do this?"

Winston nodded. Dianne sighed and pressed the delete button. "Now I just want my kids back safe and sound," she muttered. "All three of them."

✳   ✳

Neri lay low in the water on the far side of the fence, watching the growing activity inside with concern. Men had been gathering, more and more of them. Boats had been put in the water. And now, a helicopter was hovering overhead. She could not hear Charley's calls anymore, just weak, low babbles of fear. What was happening? And where were her friends?

In the mangrove swamp, Jodie lost her footing, grabbed at Daggy, and they both sprawled face first into the murky, brackish water. Jodie came up spluttering and wailing. "My hair! My makeup! It's all ruined!"

Daggy looked at her, critically. "Actually, you know, I think you look a lot better without all that paint on you."

"Do you?" Jodie regarded him in turn. "Well, now you mention it, you don't look too bad yourself messed up a bit. Sort of rugged in a daggy kind of way."

"Yeah? That's the first time a girl's ever said that to me." But then he realized she wasn't listening. She was looking at something over his shoulder.

He turned and saw a thick metal stanchion driven into the ground. Connected to it was the end of the electric fence, extending out toward the bay.

"Cables!" on the other side of the bay, Brett and Vanessa shouted simultaneously and ran over to where the thick insulated pipes were snaking along the ground.

"It's easy from here," Brett crowed. "Just follow them toward the sea and they'll lead us right to the fence!"

"Don't you think I figured that out for myself, Einstein?" Vanessa scoffed. They hurried off, following the trail, still arguing over which of them had seen it first.

✳   ✳

In the UBRI laboratory, Johannson was watching the monitors when he became aware of the little figure standing in the doorway. He turned to see Zoe, smiling at him cheekily. "Who the devil are you? And how did you get in here?" he demanded, moving toward her. Zoe let him approach and then darted back out the door. Johannson hurried after her. He got out into the corridor just in time to see her run into the cleaner's cupboard and slam the door. He walked steadily up to it and pulled it open. The light wasn't working, but in the semidarkness, he could make out the shoulder of an *ORCA* uniform jacket behind some boxes at the far side of the little room. He went over and grabbed it, only to find it was empty, propped on the back of a chair. Zoe suddenly appeared behind him. "Sucker!" she cried as she dashed back out the door.

Jason and the others, running from the lab opposite, dragged the door shut. Lee started to wedge a broken broomstick between the handle and the door jamb, sealing it shut, as Johannson made futile efforts to pull it open again from inside.

"We'll finish this," Jason said to Froggy. "You go and work out how to turn that power plant off." Froggy and Zoe headed back to the main laboratory.

They walked in the door and stopped aghast. It was not empty, as they had expected. Billy Neilson stood between them and the power plant, frowning, alerted buy the ruckus outside.

"Hey, I know you. You're *ORCA* kids. What do you think you're up to?"

To Zoe's astonishment, Froggy took a couple of steps forward, beginning to roll up his sleeves. "We're here to set that whale loose, pal. And if you try to stop us, I'm going to have to spread you all over that wall."

"Froggy!" Zoe exclaimed, impressed.

Jason and Lee came running in, having secured the cupboard door. But Billy was already stepping aside without an argument.

"I'm not going to stop you," he said. "The reason I stayed behind is because I didn't want to be part of what they're going to do to him. I might be a thief, but I draw the line somewhere."

They hesitated for a second.

"Well, come on, hurry!" Billy urged. "Once they get that probe in, he's done for. So make it fast!"

"What controls power to the net?" Jason asked.

Billy pointed. "Red button on the left."

Froggy got to it first and hit it. With a whine, the

power plant rapidly wound down and died.

Jason pulled out his pocket communicator and held it to his mouth. "Are you guys there?" There were two replies. "Now!" Jason yelled. "Cut the fence now!"

On both sides of the bay, laser cutters began to slice through the main cables like butter.

The combined UBRI forces had managed to corner Charley. With Zodiac dinghies on either side and the helicopter above, the already weakened whale had run out of fight. Hellegren was moving in on the main boat, with the probe in readiness.

Neri watched, powerless to stop it. No, no, no.

Suddenly, Hellegren heard the report as the cables snapped, sending a sound like a cannon shot echoing across the water. For a moment, the fence seemed to hover in place. Then with a groan of twisting metal it crashed into the sea and sank.

On either side of the bay, the two groups danced jigs of triumphant jubilation. Daggy and Jodie threw their arms around each other.

"I did something right!" Daggy yelled. "I'm not just a dag anymore!"

Vanessa even hugged Brett until they both realized what they were doing and quickly jumped apart.

"Let's just forget that ever happened," Brett said stiffly.

Here, Charley, Neri called. *I am here. Come to me now.*

194

With a last burst of effort, the whale suddenly made a charge. Scattering the surrounding boats like toys, it cleared a path and drove through it, racing for the mouth of the bay. Neri came to meet him and then turned, guiding him out toward deeper water.

The UBRI vessels, in total disarray, had no chance of attempting pursuit. Even the helicopter, which followed for a short distance, quickly gave up the chase as futile.

Neri and Charley, side by side, dived together, sliding beneath the surface and heading for the open sea.

CHAPTER SEVENTEEN
SIREN CALL

In the chaos following the disappearance of Charley, nobody paid any attention to the boat that slipped away from its moorings in a nearby inlet and set out to sea with its full complement of crew safely back on board.

On the way back to *ORCA*, the boat was the scene of loud and triumphant celebration. Ragged cheers split the air, palms were smacked together in recognition of mutual victory, and tales of daring became more exaggerated with each telling.

There was a moment of seriousness when Vanessa got up to make a speech.

"Try and stop her," Brett muttered out of the corner of his mouth.

Since the truth about Neri was now their secret,

she insisted, each and all should take an oath never to reveal it to anyone not already in the know. This was duly agreed to, and the party carried on as before.

But the mood abruptly changed when they arrived home. The main elevator doors opened to reveal Lucas, waiting for them, stony faced. He crooked a forefinger, told them to follow him, and led them to an empty meeting room in the officer's quarters. There, he demanded to know where they had been. He had received a message from the mainland, he said. Something about vandalism at a scientific institution and rumors of the involvement of kids from the *ORCA* base. He wanted the truth.

Jason started to tell Lucas. When he mentioned Neri's name, several of the others, horrified, moved to stop him, but he brushed them aside.

"There's no point," he said, "Mom told me he already knows about her." He outlined the day's events. "UBRI isn't going to make any big deal out of it," he finished. "If they did, someone might start asking questions about why they had a protected species cooped up in that bay."

Lucas dismissed the rest of them to face the wrath of their own parents before confronting Lee.

"It's the sort of thing I might expect from some of those other kids, but you! I thought I'd raised you with a proper sense of duty. Do you realize what risks you took?"

Lee looked her father straight in the eye. "Yes, Dad. And I'd take them again if I had to."

Lucas was struck speechless. Lee had never spoken to him this way before.

"I'm sorry," she went on, "I know what my duty means to you, but sometimes there are things more important than that. And one of them's Neri. This is her territory. She belongs here and so does that whale. No one's got the right to take either of them away and put them in a cage. They're part of the ocean. And isn't protecting the ocean why *ORCA*'s here in the first place?"

Lucas didn't reply. He simply sat, looking at his daughter, deep in thought.

✳   ✳

"I can't believe you boys just went off like that without telling me!" Dianne was saying. As she continued the lecture, Winston walked to the fax machine where a message was printing out. He ripped it off, looked at it and pondered for a moment. Then he carefully folded it and put it in his pocket.

Dianne was starting to run out of steam. "What you did was stupid and dangerous and you must never ever do anything like it again." There was a brief pause, then she added, "But hopefully, you'll never have to." And she told them about erasing all trace of Neri from their files.

When she had finished, Jason came over to her, followed by Brett. "We know what it meant to you, Mom," Jason said quietly and, a little awkwardly, he hugged her. She put an arm around each of their shoulders. "Not as much as you two do," she replied, "or her, if it comes to that."

Then she quickly cuffed both of them across the back of the head. "Just in case you think I'm going soppy," she explained.

"Dr. Bates." They looked over to see Lucas standing in the doorway. "I thought I should tell you I've decided against filing that report. In fact, if anyone asks, I've never seen any of your research. Is that understood?"

"Perfectly, Commander," she smiled. He turned to go. "And Jack . . ." He reacted to the unfamiliar use of his name. ". . . Thanks." He nodded and left.

"But Mom, this means you've destroyed your files for nothing," Jason pointed out.

She shook her head. "I would've had to, anyway. Neri would never have been safe with them around. At least this way, she's free to make a choice. Do you know where she is?"

"She'll be at the island."

"Take me there. I think I can be trusted now, don't you? Let's see if she wants to come home."

As they headed out, Winston hurried to bring up the rear.

✳   ✳

Neri stood on the beach facing them, a southerly breeze ruffling her hair.

199

"Don't you understand, Neri?" Dianne said, "You can live with us, as part of the family."

Brett grinned. "Hey, we're a bit on the crazy side, but you get used to us."

Neri's eyes filled with sadness. "There are many good things in your world. And I love my family. But I must go."

"Go? Go where?" Jason asked.

Neri looked out toward the cove. There was a great spout of water and then Charley breached. "On the long voyage with him."

Dianne grasped it first. "The migration? Neri, you can't."

"I must. That is the way of my world."

She walked over to Winston, and embraced him clumsily. "Good friend. Watch for me in the sea."

"There should be a wise old saying to cover this situation," he commented, "but somehow, it escapes me right now."

Then she turned to Dianne. "Farewell, Mother."

Dianne clutched her and held her tight. "You can't leave, Neri."

Winston's voice was soft but strangely firm. "Dianne, let her go."

Dianne slowly relinquished her grip and Neri moved on to Brett. "Remember, no eating badberries," she whispered in his ear.

Finally she stood facing Jason. As they embraced, their lips brushed for a moment. When she pulled away, Neri frowned. She reached up and felt something on her cheek, then looked at her hand in confusion.

"Hey, Neri," Brett said, "that's the only time I've ever seen you cry."

Charley breached again out in the bay. Neri heard his song. "He tells me to come now."

She stepped back, took one last look at them all, then ran down the sand and disappeared into the sea.

Dianne's voice broke the silence. "How do we know she's ever going to come back?"

"I have good reason to think she will," Winston said. "I chose not to show you this until certain decisions were reached. Just in case scientific curiosity should cloud your judgment."

He reached into his pocket and pulled out the folded fax. Dianne opened it and started to read.

"It's from the pathologist on the mainland," Winston said casually. "He tested Neri's blood. It isn't human. In fact, it contains DNA structures never seen on this planet before."

Jason's head swam. When he first met Neri, she had called the whale Jali. Was this some other half-remembered language, one not spoken anywhere on earth? He had scoffed at the idea of her being a mermaid, but could she be something even more fantastic? Until that moment, everything had seemed explained by the wreckage of the boat in the Badlands. But now he thought—what if it wasn't a boat? What kind of craft was it that had brought Neri into their lives?

He heard Mom echoing his thoughts. "If she isn't human, then where did she come from?"

"I don't know," Winston admitted, "but I suspect the answer lies somewhere on this island. And one day, she will have to return to find out for herself."

Out to sea, Neri surfaced beside Charley. She lifted one arm in a last good-bye. "Watch for me!" she called.

Then the great flukes of Charley's tail came up, she arched beside him, and they slowly vanished together into the world beneath the ocean.